SURFBOARD STABBING

Charlotte Gibson Mysteries #7

JASMINE WEBB

Chapter 1

My surfboard cut across the water like a razor blade, arcing beautifully along the fifteen-foot wave. I was Carissa Moore, Hawaii's hometown hero and one of the best surfers of all time.

"Next stop, the Olympics," I shouted triumphantly as I lost my balance. My weight shifted over the board a few times as I tried to stay on, rocking me from side to side, but it was no use. I let out a yelp, fell to the side, smacked the water like a breeching humpback whale, and a couple of seconds later, I came spluttering back up to the surface, just in time for my fiberglass surfboard to bump me on the head.

Great.

"That was a good start, but the Olympics might be a few years away still," Zoe said, wading toward me in the two feet of water near the shore. "You stayed on the board for at least four seconds that time, though. That's an improvement."

"Did you see that wave? It was at least fifteen feet high," I said, motioning to the water. Of course, looking at the waves now, I could see that in reality even the biggest were struggling to break the two foot mark. We were at the Cove, known as being one of the best spots for beginners to learn to surf in Kihei.

"Yes, at least," Zoe said with a disbelieving smile.

I scowled. "This was a stupid idea."

"It was your idea."

"That doesn't mean it can't be stupid."

"I totally agree, and I told you that entering a surfing competition when you don't know how to surf, just because you wanted an entry to the prize raffle, was a bad idea."

"You let me register," I pointed out.

"That's because you're an adult. If you want to make your own bad decisions, I can't stop you. I'm your best friend, not your mother."

I sighed, sitting on the sand, the water reaching my chest, my surfboard bobbing a few feet away, attached to my ankle by the leash, letting myself be gently rocked by the movement of the water. "This was a dumb idea."

"You could always be a no-show on competition

day," Zoe pointed out. "You'd lose your entry fee, but you'd keep your dignity."

"But then I wouldn't be entered in the prize drawing. And I want that one year's supply of free pie."

Zoe laughed. "You're an adult. You have a job. You can buy yourself pie."

"Nope, free pie tastes better than pie you've paid for. That's how science works."

"That... is not at all how science works."

"It definitely is. Just because it hasn't caught up to reality yet doesn't make me wrong. I'm going to win that year of free pie. And I'm going to try not to humiliate myself too much in the process."

A month ago, registrations had opened up for the annual Maui Pineapple Express Surfing Competition. Zoe, an avid amateur surfer, competed every year, and she had brought home the flyer one day. The closest I'd come to surfing was a disastrous attempt at stand-up paddleboard yoga, which I only did to try and find a killer, since I did my best to avoid the ocean at all costs, but when Zoe brought home the flyer for a local surf competition, I was instantly attracted to the advertised raffle prizes. Especially the raffle prize offering a year of free pie.

When I'd questioned Zoe and found out all someone had to do to enter the contest was register and compete, I was in.

Of course, the fact that I had no idea how to

surf was just a minor detail. I only had to try; I didn't have to win. But I still didn't want to totally humiliate myself, so Zoe had spent her spare time in the last two weeks teaching me the basics of standing up on a surfboard.

And every time I got up on that surfboard, I felt as if I was taking on Jaws, the massive surf break on the north shore of Hawaii, commonly known as the biggest wave in the world. A few times, Zoe had taken video of me so I could see what I was doing wrong (spoiler alert: everything). And in reality, the waves I was taking on were less Jaws and more Nibbled-on-by-a-Goldfish.

"Okay. Do you want to get back on the board and try again?" Zoe asked.

"No," I replied sulkily. "I'm done for today. Tomorrow is the big day, and let's face it. I'm not going to become world class in that time."

"You're not, because you have devoted something like seven hours to this sport in your entire life. You're still a few short of that ten thousand."

"Well, thank you for trying to make me less of an embarrassment, at least."

"My pleasure. And relax. You're not going to embarrass yourself. I mean, sure, you have no idea what you're doing, but as long as you're out there having fun, that's the main thing."

"I'm sitting in the water having a temper tantrum and every time I get on that board, I end up belly flopping into the ocean. I'm pretty sure I have a concussion from my surfboard hitting me in the head—not that I can blame it, there's sand inside parts of me I didn't even know existed, and I don't know if I'm crying from the saltwater in my eyes or because I'm so bad at this."

"But you do get to complain, and that is one of your favorite things in the world."

"That's true," I conceded. "Still, I think I've done enough for one day. Enough for a lifetime. Tomorrow is the first day of heats. I'm going to get immediately steamrolled by everyone in the amateur women's nineteen-to-twenty-nine category, including you, and then I never have to step on another surfboard again. And I can drown my sorrows in free pie."

"You haven't won the raffle yet. You do realize that, right?" Zoe pointed out.

"I'm manifesting the win. The universe owes me. If it's making me get on a surfboard, it owes me free pie."

"Okay," Zoe said with a laugh. "Well, in that case, let's get out of here. I have a shift at the hospital to cover tonight. Mark was nice enough to swap with me so I can compete tomorrow."

"Do you know who else is in our category?"

"I know there's Elise Jones, since I saw her a few days ago and spoke to her about it. A few of the other regulars. But other than that, I have no idea."

"Do you think you're going to defend your title?" I asked with a grin.

"I hope so. It's my last year in the nineteen-to-twenty-nine age group, so I'm going to do my best to hang onto that title for one last time."

"And then we join the old-people-over-thirty category. I'm going to have to start signing my texts and squinting at the screen when I look at my phone."

Zoe chuckled. "Don't let Dot and Rosie hear you say that."

"True. They'd probably murder me in my sleep."

I got up and walked toward the beach, pulling the board along by the leash instead of carrying it until we reached the shore, where I finally picked it up. Surfboards were huge and unwieldy. At least this one was.

"On the bright side, the weather looks good for tomorrow. There should be a nice surge. The waves will be bigger than what you're used to, but I know you can handle it."

"I can. I'm basically a professional now," I said, knowing full well it was a lie.

"Right," Zoe said with a laugh. "Come on, champ."

I followed my best friend as we walked back to our shared apartment. Tomorrow, it was competition time. I didn't currently have any cases to investigate. This was my moment.

Not to win the whole thing. Even I wasn't that deluded; I was cheering for Zoe to win our category. But I was cheering for myself to win that free pie.

Chapter 2

I woke up early the following morning, well before the sun was due to make an appearance. Another reason to dislike surfing: the early starts. A lump rose in my throat. All of a sudden, in the cold, hard light of day, this didn't seem like the best idea ever anymore.

What was wrong with me? I had no idea what I was doing. I didn't like surfing. That had been Dad's thing, not mine.

Thinking about him gave rise to a small pang in my chest. He would have been so proud of me if he could have seen me on the water. It wouldn't have mattered to him that half the time, when I tried to get up on the board, I failed and fell over. It wouldn't have mattered to him that I'd mastered the art of the belly flop much better than I had the bottom turn. It wouldn't have mattered to him that

I often forgot to lift myself up when a wave came toward me while I was swimming out, and it would crash over me as if I was George Clooney's fishing boat in *A Perfect Storm*.

No, I knew Dad was watching from up above, cheering me on like I was the best surfer in the world. But even knowing that, I couldn't get past the fact that there was nothing about being in the ocean that I liked. And I was not good at it. But today, I was going to go out there, and I was going to surf. In public. With people watching. In a competition Carissa Moore had entered. That's right, five-time world champion and Olympic gold medalist, Carissa Moore. Luckily, there was a pro category, so we wouldn't actually be going up against each other head-to-head.

I didn't belong here. A month ago, throwing my name into the ring—or the ocean—on a whim so I could maybe win a year of free pie in a raffle had sounded like a good idea at the time, but now that the day had actually arrived, I was much more nervous about it.

I got up and headed out into the kitchen, where Coco, my small dog, was inhaling her breakfast. Zoe had fed her and prepared breakfast for both of us: a bagel smeared with a generous serving of cream cheese with a side of scrambled eggs and some Greek yogurt with local honey.

"I feel like I'm going to throw up," I admitted. "This was a bad idea."

"Well that's the last time I cook you breakfast," Zoe joked. "I don't know. At the very least, you've learned a new skill. And possibly a fun life lesson. Besides, I said it yesterday and I'll say it again: you don't have to go through with this."

I shook my head. "I do. I signed up for this. You told me this was a bad idea, and it probably was, but I wet this bed, and now I have to lie in it."

"That's not how that expression goes."

"It's how that expression feels to me right now."

"All right," Zoe said with a grin, pushing the plate toward me. "Well, you're probably not going to actually puke, so try and get some food into you. We have a big day ahead of us."

I picked up half the bagel and began nibbling away at the edge. "Do you know what tricks you're going to do?"

"I've been working on a few, but of course, it's going to depend on the waves I catch. But I've been working on my snap for a couple of months. I realized I wasn't pushing away from the board with my back leg once I was halfway up the crest, and since I've been focusing on that, I feel like it's gotten a lot stronger. Also, I'd love to be able to do a 360. I've never tried one in competition before, but it's risky, because I'm not great at it yet."

"Oh, please. You would say that if you can't get

it exactly right ninety-nine times out of a hundred. You know who doesn't win competitions? People who play it safe."

"Also people who fall over on their boards because they tried a trick that was a little bit too far outside of their skill set, and don't end up hitting a good wave in the thirty minutes," Zoe replied.

"Sure. But what would you regret more? Losing because you played it safe and someone else beat you, knowing that you *could* have tried the 360 but didn't have the guts, or losing because you tried something cool and it didn't work out?"

"That's surprisingly insightful, especially coming from someone who's been complaining about entering this competition for the past two weeks."

"Thank you. I stole the basic idea of it from the movie *Dodgeball*."

Zoe laughed. "That makes sense. But you're right. And I keep telling myself that this is no different from any other year. That I just need to go out there and do my best, and if that's good enough to win the trophy, then great. And if it isn't, well, it means I need to work harder next year. But I want this, Charlie. I really do. It's the last time I get to claim this trophy for my age group. I've won it three times, though I wasn't around every year. When I was in college, I missed it a lot."

"Would you like me to do my best Tonya Harding on the competition?" I offered.

"Absolutely not."

I shrugged. "Just a suggestion. I'm sure Rosie would help, too."

"I'm happy to take on any suggestions that don't involve you committing a crime on my behalf. Besides, I don't want to win because the rest of the field has broken patellas. I want to win because I'm the best in the field. I want to earn it."

"You will," I said confidently. "I know you will. You're a marvel."

"Thanks. It's nice to know you have my back."

"Always. And I'm not just saying it. I've seen you out there, surfing with everyone else on this island who's obsessed with the sport. You're always one of the best."

"Let's hope today I can be too."

I knew Zoe would.

As soon as we finished breakfast, the two of us headed out, much to Coco's chagrin. We loaded up the boards in the back of Queenie, my Jeep, then hopped in and started driving to Ho'okipa Beach on the North Shore. Maui's surfing mecca was a place for more experienced riders, and I had to admit I was a bit nervous about getting into the water there.

It was going to be way more of an adventure than the Cove, a protected stretch of beach with waves suitable for beginners. Ho'okipa was where all the serious professionals went to surf, and I was well aware that it could be dangerous.

"Is Jake coming?" Zoe asked.

I shook my head. "No. He wanted to, but I asked him not to. I need to keep up this air of being great at everything that I do, and if he sees me on a surfboard, it'll shatter that mystique."

Zoe snorted. "I'm pretty sure that mystique is long gone. Did you really tell him he can't come today?"

"Yeah. Besides, he had to work."

"Oh, please. I've seen the way you two look at each other. He would have found someone to cover his shift. You have to actually let Jake into your life. I'm glad he's respected your decision, but you need to open up. I know that's hard for you, and you tend not to trust people, but if you close yourself off from him even now, when the two of you are dating, your relationship is doomed."

I shrugged. "I'm not the open-up-and-talk-about-my-feelings type. You know that."

"I do. But this isn't feelings. This is about letting your boyfriend come and see you try not to embarrass yourself on a surfboard so you can potentially win a raffle for free pie. There's nothing weird about that. Not by your standards, anyway."

"But I suck at it," I whined.

"He's not going to break up with you because you're bad at surfing. Believe me, Jake knows."

"Yeah."

Zoe glanced over at me from the passenger seat. "You're worried about screwing this up, aren't you?"

"Just a little bit. And I hate that I feel like this. I don't normally care. I'm not a serious-relationship person. I'm a go-out-with-them-once-find-out-they're-weirdos-and-pretend-I-moved-to-another-state person."

"Well, the best advice I can offer is to let Jake in. You don't have to tell him your biggest secrets. In fact, given as he's a cop, I probably wouldn't, because I have a feeling they're probably not all legal. But let him into your life. More than just the occasional dinner and then spending the night at his apartment. I bet he would love to be here today, watching you do something silly just because you have a small chance at free pie. You don't have to be perfect in front of him, because if you aren't, and he runs away, it means he doesn't deserve you."

"He doesn't deserve me?"

"Exactly. Love is about finding someone who accepts you for you. You shouldn't have to hide who you are. You're a wonderful person, Charlie. A weird one, sure. But loveable weird. Not creepy weird. I wouldn't change a single thing about you for the world. And if someone you're with doesn't appreciate you for who you are—the good and the

15

bad—then they don't deserve to be with you. Because *you* deserve to be happy, and that means being with someone who sees you for who you are."

"I think Jake is that person," I said quietly.

"Of course he is. I knew the instant he showed up to take you to a gun range and you were dressed like War Crimes Barbie that he was that person for you. He didn't even blink, when most men would have run away screaming. They *certainly* wouldn't have followed through and actually taken you to the range looking like that."

"I mean, I'm pretty sure he partly did it knowing I was also embarrassed about looking like that."

"I hope so. But the fact is, he has already seen you at your weirdest. The two of you dating is new, but he knows who you are. Don't be afraid to let him in a little bit more."

"Fine. Well, if I qualify for the finals tomorrow, I guess he can come."

"You never know," Zoe said, a small smile flittering onto her lips.

"Oh, don't be ridiculous. We both know I could have the run of my life and everyone else could fall off their boards, and I still wouldn't make those finals."

"Hey, I'm trying to be supportive here," Zoe replied with a laugh.

"And I appreciate it," I said with a grin. "I can't believe you normally get up this early to do this."

"The waves are at their best in the morning. And we want to be able to warm up and still see the experts."

"Yeah. It's been a while since I've seen pro surfers."

"They're so impressive. I love it."

I pulled into the parking lot at Ho'okipa Beach, which was already quite full. The sun was set to rise in about thirty minutes, but the beach was already bustling.

Feather flags blew in the wind, each imprinted with the competition name.

Aloha Ice Cream presents the Pineapple Express Surfing Competition 2023.

The covered picnic tables near the bathrooms had been commandeered by the organizers, who were handing out race packs to competitors. Behind them, a group of guys was working on the sound system, trying to figure out how to plug in the cables to get everything going.

Zoe and I joined the line, and when we got to the front, I instantly recognized the woman working behind the table. "Vesper!"

The woman looked up at us and grinned. "I saw your names on the sign-up sheet. Zoe, I'm not surprised about. But you, Charlie? I'm impressed. I didn't think surfing was your thing."

"It's not," I admitted. "But you know, I'm always up for trying new things."

"Right," Vesper said, a glimmer in her eye revealing that she had an indication as to the true motive behind my entering. "Well, I'm glad to see you both. I've got your bags here. We have rash guards for sale if you didn't bring one. You'll want to get out in the water and warm up before the competition begins. The first surfer drops in at eight o'clock on the dot. The professional categories are running first. Women, then men. After that, it's the open categories, which is you. Women nineteen to twenty-nine are scheduled for 11:20."

"I didn't realize you were working here today," Zoe said warmly. "Are you going to get in the water?"

"Sure am. I'm about to wrap up here, and then I figured I'd catch a few waves before things get underway. I'll see you out there while you're warming up. I don't compete anymore, but I'm still happy to send it when I get the chance."

"We'll see you soon, then," Zoe said with a smile.

I grabbed my bag and flashed her a grin then headed off.

"Cool," I said, rifling through the stuff. "There's a water bottle in here."

"Good. Maybe it'll convince you to drink more than two ounces of water a day," Zoe teased.

I stuck my tongue out at her as we headed back to Queenie to grab our boards. "How are we supposed to warm up? It's still dark out," I complained.

"It's getting lighter. Besides, this is the best time of day to surf. You get to greet the sun while you're on the water, and the waves are at their best. Come on, let's go."

"And when the sharks are at their hungriest," I grumbled, but Zoe was already out of earshot.

Zoe and I had put our swim gear on at home, so we took off our outer layers and threw them into the back of the Jeep, grabbed our towels and boards, and headed down to the water.

I took one look at the waves breaking on the beach and stopped in my tracks. "Hey, Zoe?"

"Yeah?"

"Next time I have an idea *this* dumb, can you please talk me out of it?"

"I did my best. It didn't work."

"You didn't try hard enough. You didn't tell me I was literally going to die if I go out there."

"You're not going to die."

"Look at those waves," I said, motioning to the water. These were monsters. A hundred feet tall at the very least. They had to be, surely. No wonder the wave known as Jaws was located here. Every single one of the waves out there looked as if it could swallow me whole and spit me out onto the shore. Because it was still mostly dark out, with just the first hint of light creeping over the horizon, the water was black, making it that much more intimidating. And the crazy thing was, there were people riding those waves.

About fifty people were on the water, most casually floating on their boards, letting the occasional wave wash over them. From time to time, one would decide to go for it and paddle aggressively to meet a wave before popping up onto their board as if it was nothing and cutting across the water, trying a couple of tricks before riding the wave back down, and casually dropping back onto their stomach, ready to paddle out again.

This was nothing like the protected waters of the Cove, with its small waves, perfect for a beginner like me. This was *real*.

"I'm going to die if I go out there," I said.

"You are not. There are lifeguards. Just stay on your board. This is what warm-up is for. You get used to the feeling of the big waves. And when you're competing, if you don't feel comfortable standing up, you don't."

"I haven't written my will out yet, but I blame you for this. I want you to know you can have none of my stuff if I die. You never warned me that this was what I was up against."

Zoe cocked an eyebrow skyward. "You have lived on Maui for nearly half your life. If you don't know what the waves in a surfing competition look like by now, that's on you. If you die out here today, I'm going to take all of your stuff just to spite you."

"Well, now I'm going to have to survive," I muttered with a huff. "Okay. You should go out and warm up properly. You want to win today, and that's more important than my life."

Zoe rolled her eyes. "It's only heats today. I just need to finish in the top eight, and I qualify for tomorrow. Come on. We'll go out together, and I'll make sure you don't drown."

I smiled at Zoe. She really was the best friend anyone could ask for.

Chapter 3

I stepped into the water and lay down on my board. Even though it was the middle of winter —the first week of February, in fact—and the sun's rays were just beginning to peek over Haleakala behind us, the water was still warm enough to swim in without a wetsuit. I trudged carefully through the waves until I got to thigh-deep water then jumped onto my board and paddled out into deeper water.

I didn't go far; the waves farther out were way too high for my liking. I was pretty sure I had just seen somebody go into a barrel. That was way, way past my skill level. I was still at the stand-up-and-hang-on-for-dear life stage.

"Enjoying the water?" a voice called out behind me. It was Vesper, paddling out confidently on her own board, prosthetic leg and all.

"'Enjoying' is a strong word," I replied.

Vesper cackled. "There's nothing in the world more freeing than being out here. Let your body become one with the ocean. This is where magic happens if you let it."

"You know where else magic happens? Solid ground."

Vesper shook her head. "Nope. Never. I've been on this earth a long time, Charlie. And let me tell you, everything interesting that has ever happened to me? It's happened out here. The ocean has a certain pull to it. An attraction."

"That's just called the tide, and it's caused by the moon."

"Aren't you hilarious. Well, I'm going to go out and catch some waves before we get started. I'm judging today. Leslie roped me into doing it. But I wanted to get some action in first."

"Please go easy on me," I begged

Vesper laughed. "I love that you're out here, Charlie. Let go of your fear, and I promise, there's a whole new world for you to explore."

With that, Vesper paddled off deeper into the water, while I bobbed up and down as the small waves passed under me.

"She's right, you know," Zoe said. "It really is a whole new world."

"I can barely handle the world that's on land. I don't need to add another one to the mix."

"Fair enough. Well, you just have to get through

today, and you never have to step on another surf-board again."

"I think I can make that happen. And if all goes right, I'll have my coupon for free pie for a year by tomorrow night."

"Sounds like a plan," Zoe said with a grin.

"You should go out and warm up on your own," I suggested. "I can handle this."

"Are you sure?"

"Yeah. I'm just going to stay around here where it's not super deep, and I probably won't drown. And if I do, at least I won't have to go through with this."

"At least you're looking on the bright side. I'll see you soon."

"Have fun!"

I watched as Zoe paddled confidently out into the deeper water, joining the fifty or so other people getting ready for the competition or just enjoying what were supposedly the best conditions of the day for surfing.

I got up on my board a couple of times but eventually decided I was just going to pretend to be a turtle for a while. I bobbed along like a *honu*, the green sea turtles that were so common on Maui and on this stretch of beach in particular. As soon as the sun came over the mountain and doused the beach in light, I knew they would make their way to the shore to enjoy a nice nap in the warm rays.

After a while, Zoe returned. "What on earth are you doing?" she asked me with a chuckle. I'd been moving my neck backward and forward over the front of my board, pretending to come in and out of my "shell."

"Being a turtle," I replied casually.

"Well, I guess now would be a great time to tell you the reason sharks accidentally feed on humans is because on our surfboards, from underneath, we look like turtles to them. A nice, tasty, snack."

I immediately snapped my arms and legs next to me, taking them out of the water so my whole body was on the board.

Zoe laughed. "Don't worry. You're in shallow enough water that you're probably not going to get eaten."

"I don't like how much work the word "probably" is doing in that sentence."

"Okay, then let's go to shore. I want to watch the professionals anyway. The first few heats should be fun."

"Cool, me too."

The two of us began paddling back toward the main beach. Without realizing it, I'd been pulled away from where we'd entered and was now a few hundred feet to the east of where we'd gone in. Whoops. I probably should have been paying a bit more attention.

As we got closer, though, I spotted someone else on their board, bobbing toward the shore.

"Hey, who's that?" I asked, squinting as I looked over at the person. "Is he okay?"

Zoe looked in the direction I was pointing, and her eyes widened. "He looks like he's in trouble."

She immediately began paddling in the direction of the man's board, and I followed her. He wasn't moving beyond the effects of the water, about twenty feet from the shore, and as we got closer, I realized why. There was a giant chef's knife sticking out of his back. It looked like a shark fin as he floated in the water on top of his surfboard.

I immediately began paddling toward him as if my life depended on it.

"Get help!" Zoe called out to me.

I nodded and jumped off my board, as the water was only about two feet deep here. I undid my leash and abandoned my board in the water then ran to the beach, waving my arms in the air. "Help! We need some help over here! Someone's been stabbed!" I shouted.

Straight away, three nearby men looked at me. Two of them paused, stunned, but the third instantly started running toward the parking lot. "I'll get the EMTs," he called back over his shoulder as he rushed off.

Because this was a competition with a professional side to it, there was an ambulance on standby, ready to take anyone who needed it to the hospital down the road in Kahului.

The other two men gathered their wits about them ran back with me toward the beach, where Zoe was bringing the body in. I knew from the way she was acting that it was too late.

"He's dead," she announced as we got close, confirming my suspicions. "Given how much blood is in the water around him, there's no chance we're bringing him back. It's over. We need to call the police."

The two men stared at the body for a second, then one nodded and pulled out his phone. "I'll call 9-1-1."

"Holy shit, that's Tony," the third man said, staring down at the body. "Someone killed Tony."

"Who is he?" I asked.

"Tony Murray. A surfing legend." The man's voice was hollow. "I can't believe it. Who would do this?"

The second man came back. "Police are on their way."

"It's Tony," the man told him.

"Tony? You're joking. Seriously?"

"Yeah."

By now, a few more people had realized something was happening and were circling the body. The EMTs had also arrived with the third man. They acted quickly, immediately carrying Tony's body onto the shore, but it quickly became obvious to them as well that Zoe had been right: he was past help.

I stepped back, letting the EMTs take over while we waited for the police.

"Someone murdered him, obviously," I said to Zoe. "I wonder who."

"It had to be someone out on the water," she replied quietly, looking at the waves.

A few of the other surfers had noticed the commotion on the shore, and most were coming in now.

"Do you know who he is? Tony?" I asked.

Zoe nodded. "Tony Murray. Local legend. He's lived on the island his whole life. Grew up in Paia, went professional for a few years, and has spent his career after his retirement in the industry. He owns a surfing company near here now that makes custom boards, and he runs a program to get local kids into the water. Doesn't charge a cent for it."

"Oh, wow."

"Yeah. Everyone in the surfing community knows Tony. Also, he's Vesper's ex-boyfriend."

"Did they end it on bad terms?"

"From what I heard, it was messy. None of that was from Vesper, mind you. I've never spoken to her about it. But there were allegations of cheating, fighting, and apparently, she threw something at him that gave him a nice scar on his forehead."

"Shit, she's going to be a suspect, then, isn't she?"

"I'm not a cop, so I can't say for sure, but I'd guess it's likely."

I ran a hand down my face. Vesper wasn't a killer. I knew that. She was a little bit crazy, sure. You had to be to lose a leg to a shark attack and still go out on the water for fun, in my opinion. But being a little nuts didn't make you a murderer.

My eyes scanned the water, looking for her. I spotted her a second later; she was just coming in now, looking confused. Her eyes scanned the crowd. I waved as they landed on me, and she came over.

"What's going on?" she asked.

At this point, we were standing far enough away from the body, and a crowd had formed around it, so Tony's body was no longer visible.

"It's Tony," Zoe said quietly. "He's been murdered."

Vesper let out a small gasp. "Tony? Really? How? Who did it?"

"We don't know. We found him floating on his board as we were coming back."

"I'd been dragged out this way a bit without realizing it," I explained. "Zoe was leading me back to shore when we saw him. Someone stabbed him."

Vesper closed her eyes. "I suppose I'm one of the few people on this island who's not going to be surprised. But who could have done it?"

"It was someone on the water," I said. "It had to be. Which means that when the police arrive, they're going to be looking at you, because the first thing everyone is going to tell them is that the two of you were in a relationship and that it ended badly."

"Yeah, it ended badly because he was a douchebag with the emotional intelligence of a cricket and an even smaller... well, never mind. Tony was one of those people who, on the surface, got along with everyone. But he was a very different person in private, and that's why things didn't work out between us. But I wouldn't have killed him. I mean, if you gave me the chance to punch him in the face, I would have taken it. But murder? No. Never."

"Maybe leave out that part about being willing to punch him in the face when the police talk to you," I said.

"In fact, do not speak to the police without a lawyer," Zoe added. "I'm going to call my mom. She'll represent you or arrange for someone to do so. The instant the police try and ask you questions, tell them you have representation, and you're not willing to speak to them without a lawyer present. And then stay quiet. I mean it. Don't say a single thing."

Vesper grinned. "I forgot your Mom's that big hotshot attorney, right?"

"She is, so trust me. I know what I'm talking about."

"And I'm going to look into this too," I said instantly. "I'm not going to let the cops nail you for this, Vesper. Not for something you didn't do."

Vesper inhaled sharply. "Shit. This is serious, isn't it?"

"Yes," I replied. "It really is. But the best way to keep you in the clear is to find out who did this. I need you to tell me everything you can about your relationship with Tony. When did it start? When did it end? Why did it end badly? And don't just tell me he had a small dick. I need the actual details if I'm going to solve his murder."

"Fine," Vesper said. "But I'm telling you, I didn't do this."

"And I believe you," I replied. "But I need to know everything I can."

Before Vesper had a chance to speak, a familiar voice behind me spoke. "You know, just once, I would love to be called to a murder and not see you all over my crime scene."

I turned around to see myself staring into the gorgeous brown eyes I knew all too well these days. It was Jake.

Chapter 4

"Jake, hello," I sang as if we had just casually met in the park. "Welcome to the crime scene. I'd like to tell you to have a nice stay, but uh, it's not the greatest situation. Zoe and I found the body, it was floating on a surfboard."

"Of course you did. Okay, stay here, will you? I need to get this place cordoned off before everyone stamps all over any evidence there might be."

I nodded and stepped back while Jake took command of the area. He was able to make his voice carry without yelling, and the people around the body quickly began moving away. Behind Jake, a handful of uniformed officers had also arrived, along with Liam, Jake's human donut of a partner.

"It's always you," Liam snarled as soon as he saw me. "You're always involved in murder cases. It's suspicious."

"Good morning to you, too," I replied. "I know it's early, and you've probably only made one stop at Krispy Kreme so far, but try rubbing those two brain cells of yours together really hard. Really make a fire with them. You might realize that I'm a private investigator. It's my job to be here. And every other murder you've ever been assigned to has been solved. By me."

Liam's brow furrowed as a confused look creased his face. "What do you mean, try and make a fire?"

Beside me, Zoe snorted.

"Yes, you're definitely just the guy to solve this case," I said sarcastically. "Just the brightest person out here."

"I know you've got something to do with all this," Liam snarled. "It's too much. It's not just a coincidence."

"Right, well, get on that, Columbo. If you find that proof that I'm a serial killer, I'll be right here waiting."

"Yo, Liam," Jake called.

Liam glared at me one more time before turning and waddling off to join his partner.

"Think he's going to be trouble?" Zoe asked quietly as he was leaving.

"Only if I turn into a honey cruller."

Zoe chuckled. "Seriously, though. You never know with someone like that. He's definitely out to get you. Just because he's not smart doesn't mean he can't cause problems for you. There are plenty of idiots in the world that have ruined lives."

"You're right. I won't underestimate him, but he has nothing on me. I happened to be here when the body was spotted. I didn't kill Tony, and he can't prove I did."

"I know. It's not Tony specifically I'm worried about. It's the future. You never know what he might do. There are crooked cops out there."

I nodded, and a chill ran down my spine. I knew Zoe was right. If Liam really did want to make my life hell, it wouldn't be *that* hard for him to do it. "I'll keep an eye on him."

"Smart. I agree, he's not going to do anything now. But I wouldn't put it past him in the future. Especially if you and Jake get closer."

"You think he's jealous?" I asked with a grin.

"I don't think he's going to be pleased about you playing an important role in the life of someone who's important in his life. The question is, how far is he going to go? Is he incompetent or vindictive?"

"Why not both?"

"It could be both, which could be even more dangerous," Zoe conceded. "But keep an eye out."

"I will." I turned to Vesper. "Do you want to answer my questions now, before Jake gets back here?"

"Sure. Yeah. Wow, this is worse than the time

the cops thought I had a secret grow op in the basement of the nursery I worked at."

"Did you?" I asked.

"No, of course not. It was in a shed out the back," Vesper replied with a wink.

"Okay, let's start with the basics. How long were you and Tony together, and when did you break up?"

"Uh, we got together… I don't know. Must have been around a year ago now. Maybe a little more. I've known him for forty years, of course. But we never saw each other romantically. Never worked out before, you know? Then, out of nowhere, he asks me out. I say sure. Why not? We start dating. And it was good to start with. I mean, okay, it was fine. Given the shape of a surfboard, you'd think he'd know his way around a certain part of a woman's anatomy a bit better."

"Oh, good, I'm regretting this conversation already," I said.

"Prude," Vesper shot back. "You're the one who wanted to know. Anyway, it had been a while since I'd gotten any from anywhere outside the drawer next to my bed, so I put up with it. And Tony was fun. He'd always been fun. That was one thing I could say about him. Even when we were kids, Tony was the guy skipping school in fourth grade, setting fireworks off from the school roof on Halloween when we were teenagers, and the kid who always had a fresh supply of weed. Sure, as he grew up, he stopped breaking the law as much, especially since with his surfing career, it risked giving him trouble when he travelled, but he was still a fun guy. We had good times."

"So what happened?"

Vesper shrugged. "After a few months, the bad times outweighed the good. Tony was secretive. He'd leave in the middle of the night and swear he was just doing some business stuff, but come on. I wasn't born yesterday. He was getting some on the side, and I wasn't going to take it. He swore to me that I was wrong, that he wasn't cheating on me. I told him it was one thing to cheat on me. It was entirely another to cheat on me and then try to gaslight me into thinking *I* was the crazy one. So I told him I was finished with him. This was about, oh, I don't know. Eight, nine months ago?"

"And it was a bit violent, your breakup?"

"Oh, I don't know about that."

"Did you or did you not throw some surfboard tools at him?" Zoe asked.

"I mean, I did. An angle grinder. But it's not like it was plugged in or anything."

"Okay, you *really* need to not talk to the police without a lawyer," Zoe said.

"And you hit him?" I asked. "Zoe said that's what caused his scar."

"Sure did," Vesper replied with a grin. "Don't

worry, I won't smile if I have to tell the cops that, either. But it was a good throw. Got him right above the eyebrow. I told him he could think of the scar as a parting gift to remember me by."

"And that was that? You left, you were broken up, and you never saw him again?"

Vesper snorted. "I wish. Tony must have realized he'd just lost the best thing he was ever going to get. He never stopped, you know. Even after I told him it was over, even after I clocked him in the head with a grinder because he didn't want to let me leave, he kept after me. He'd call me twenty times a day. Park in the visitor's spot outside our building."

I snapped my fingers. "Right. I actually remember seeing him a few times, now that you say that. I thought it was weird that he would just sit there in the car, but I figured he was waiting for someone."

"Yeah, for me. Whenever I came home, he'd try and get me to change my mind. He'd swear he wasn't seeing anyone else, that it was just work, and that he wanted to be with me. Blah, blah, blah. I told him he wasn't good enough in bed for me to risk that he was lying to me again. Then I told him if he didn't leave me alone, I was going to wait until he fell asleep in that car one night and drop a match into the fuel tank. He got the hint."

"Again, things you're absolutely not going to tell the police," Zoe said, her eyes widening.

"Don't worry, honey. This isn't my first rodeo," Vesper said with a knowing smile.

"Okay. In that case, do you know if Tony was still single? Did he have another girlfriend? Maybe the woman he was cheating on you with?"

"Always. Tony was one of those guys who couldn't handle being single. He always needed to be in a relationship. It was one of the reasons I was a bit hesitant to get with him before and why I never did it when I was younger. He's been like that since he was a teenager. He had a wandering eye, and he got bored easily. Silly me. I thought as soon as we were actually together, he'd realize there was nothing better out there. But I was wrong. I just had to be strong enough to kick him to the curb when he finally got tired of me. Which I did."

"So that means there should be a few other exes out there who might have something against him," I said. "At least that opens up the suspect field a bit. How many women has he been with since you?"

"Just Lily," Vesper said. "They've actually been together for a while now; nearly eight months. Officially. I have a sneaking suspicion she's the one Tony was cheating on me with, since they announced they were a couple about two weeks after we broke up."

"That's a decent length relationship if they've been together that long now," I said.

"Yeah. Well, it helps that she's twenty-four. From his side, at least. And she gave him a kidney."

"She *what*?" I asked, incredulous.

"Tony's had issues with his for decades. A couple years ago, it got really bad, and he started going into kidney failure. He had to go to the hospital for dialysis regularly. He was on a transplant list. Everyone in the surfing world knew that. But just after they started dating, Lily got herself tested. It was a long shot, of course."

"Yes. With kidney transplants, the best odds at finding a match are with a family member," Zoe said.

"And Tony didn't have any family. No brothers or sisters, cousins, or anything like that. So he had to rely on a stranger," Vesper continued. "Lily had the same blood type as he did."

"It would have had to be more than that, too. Blood type is important, but it's not the only factor," Zoe explained. "Tissue typing, called HLA, is arguably even more important than blood type. There are essentially twelve different types of tissue, and the closer to a 12/12 match, the better the odds that a transplant will be successful. There are a couple other things that need to be checked as well, but that's the main one."

Vesper nodded. "That must have been it, then. I don't know the details, but I know about six months ago, Tony got a transplant from Lily."

"That's pretty quick after they started dating," I

said, raising my eyebrows. "Only a couple of months?"

"Yeah. She's young and in love. I guess she doesn't have the life experience to know that ultimately, men are the worst, and it's one thing to give them your hand in marriage, but a kidney is so much more than that," Vesper said, shaking her head. "You can always divorce a guy, but you can't get your organs back from them. I feel bad for her, really."

Her eyes moved over to the edge of the beach, where one of the EMTs was caring for Lily. She was sitting on the ground, staring away into nothing.

"Can she get her kidney back now, at least?" I asked, looking at the body.

"No," Zoe replied. "That's not how it works. For one thing, a transplant is a massively invasive procedure."

"So is losing a kidney," I pointed out.

"Yes. But one invasive procedure is better than two. Besides, human beings generally live a normal life with just one kidney. It shouldn't affect Lily's life span or quality of life at all, but the risks involved in taking a kidney back out of Tony and putting it into her are real."

"Okay. As much as I am interested in the details of why Lily can't get her kidney back from her dead boyfriend—and believe me, I am—right now I'm more interested in who could have killed him," I said. "Who else is there on the water that Tony would have had a beef with?"

Vesper shrugged. "Honestly, I don't know. I don't think there were a lot of people. Tony was a legend on this island. Everyone loved him. You had to really get to know him to see his flaws. He's one of those people who on the outside, he had more charisma than Freddie Mercury. He got along with everyone. He ran a charity that got kids out onto the water for free."

"So who knew him well enough to know what was underneath?"

"Well, anyone who used to be with him. Or is. Lily, of course. But she's obviously broken up about it, and she loved him enough that she gave him a kidney. And then there's me. Kamalani dated him about five years ago, and she's here today, but she wasn't on the water. She's one of the organizers. I'm sure she's around. Besides, no way she killed him. She's long since moved on; she's happily married now. She's totally over him. The only other person I can think of is his business partner, Daniel Yang."

"Issues at work?"

"Well, that's the thing. I haven't heard of any. As far as I know, business was booming. But you never know, do you? That's him there."

Vesper pointed to a man standing at the edge of the crowd, speaking to a couple of other men. He was about five foot eleven, slim, but with the toned shoulders and legs of someone who spent much of their free time surfing. Water dripped slowly from his short black hair and onto his shoulders; he had obviously been in the water when Tony was killed.

I nodded. "Okay. Anyone else you can think of?"

Vesper shook her head. "Sorry. As I said, Tony was a legend. Most people out here love the guy."

At that moment, out of the corner of my eye, I spotted Liam strutting over, followed closely by Jake.

"Here come the cops," I muttered.

Chapter 5

"Vesper Novak," Liam growled in her direction. "We meet again. We heard you used to be in a relationship with Tony, our victim."

"If you know me so well, then you know the next words coming out of my mouth: lawyer. I'm not talking to you without one," Vesper replied.

"Oh, come on. You don't have to be like that," Liam replied, doing his best impression of a decent human being and failing miserably. "We're just looking for information about Tony, and we were told you might have some. You're not under arrest right now. You can move around as you want."

"Gee, thanks. Do I get to take a piss without asking your permission first?" Vesper replied. "I said what I said. I'm not talking to you without a lawyer."

"We can't interview her right now, Liam," Jake said, putting a firm hand on his partner's arm.

Liam narrowed his eyes at Vesper. "You know who talks to lawyers? People who have something to hide."

"Or people who are afraid of being railroaded by lazy cops who are more interested in making an arrest than actually bringing the real criminal to justice," I replied, crossing my arms.

"Charlie, can I talk to you in private for a second?" Jake asked.

I nodded, and the two of us walked about fifteen feet away from the others.

"What's your take on this? Off the record. Are you working this case?"

"Yeah, I'm working it. I trust you, believe me, but I don't trust Liam. And this is Vesper's life we're talking about. We both know she's a suspect. She and Tony broke up less than a year ago."

"And she's the reason he's got a scar above his eyebrow."

"No comment."

"Look, I need you to stay out of the way on this."

"What makes you think I won't? I'm running my own separate investigation."

"Yeah. Don't worry, I get that you're going to do this, even if I think it's a bad idea."

"Good. Is this your way of telling me you don't think we can work together?"

"No. It's my way of telling you that I don't want you to stay on Liam's bad side."

"He only has bad sides."

Jake shot me a look, and I held my hands up in front of me. "Fine. I'll make an effort to avoid him. Is that enough?"

"It is. Thank you. And look, I know this is the first case we're working simultaneously since we started dating. We have the same goal here. We want to bring a killer to justice. We're coming at this separately, but I don't think we need to be antagonistic."

"I agree," I replied. "Your partner doesn't, though. So I will stay away from him. And from you. I'll find the killer by myself, and then Liam will have another reason to think I'm secretly a serial killer who's committing all these crimes by myself and he's going to stop me. You really need to get him to stop watching *NCIS* or whatever dumb show he's getting all these ideas from."

Jake sighed. "I'll try. Look, I know Vesper won't talk to me without a lawyer, but is there anything she's told you that you think could help? Off the record."

"Not unless you think it'll help to know that sleeping with Tony was like being with an excited seal flopping across the beach."

"Well, that's a mental image I'm never going to be able to erase from my brain."

"They were exes. They broke up months ago. Vesper didn't do this, Jake. You know her."

"I do, and that's why I'm not eliminating her from the suspect list. Believe me, I would love to. She's my neighbor too. But I have to look at this rationally."

"And you're saying I'm not?" I asked, narrowing my eyes.

"Well, you're automatically eliminating her just because you know and like her."

"I'm eliminating her because I don't think she did this. But I'm not going to be irrational about it. If it turns out Vesper did kill Tony, I want her in jail just as much as you do. I'm going to go where the evidence takes me. But I'm also not going to automatically pillory our neighbor just because she dated the wrong guy."

"I'm not going to pillory her. I'm just trying to get to the truth, no matter what it is. And sometimes, that means having to talk to people I know and like. Besides, it's not as if Vesper hasn't got a history with the law."

"Let me guess: she got caught with joints a few times, and now everyone at the Maui PD thinks she's a hardened criminal."

"Of course not. I mean yes, she's been caught

with some joints. And also, she was the prime suspect for some worse stuff back in the eighties."

"That was never proven."

"No."

"But you're still going to hold it against her."

"I'm not, no."

"Then why mention it?"

Jake ran a hand across his face. "Because it all matters. The justice system isn't perfect. We both know that. It would be nice if it was, but sometimes, we know someone committed a crime and just can't prove it in a court of law."

"So you're going to use it against them thirty years later and suspect them of another crime?"

"I haven't got any suspects yet. I don't have enough information. But nothing happens in a vacuum. If OJ was suspected of a murder, yeah, I would probably factor in his history, even if, technically, there's no murder on his rap sheet. But I am going to give Vesper a fair shot. If she didn't do this, I'm not going to railroad her into a false conviction."

"Good. Then we both have the same goal: finding the killer, no matter who they are. The difference is I just don't believe it's one of the people we live thirty feet from."

"Then we're on the same page."

"Yes."

Electricity crackled between us, but it was

different to the usual spark of attraction I felt with Jake. This was the adversarial type, because we both had the same goals but were going to use different tactics to reach them. I didn't believe Vesper was the killer. I was sure she wasn't. And I was going to find out who it really was.

"And listen, I don't want to have to do this, but I have to cancel dinner," Jake said apologetically.

I waved a hand. "Don't worry about it. I totally understand."

"Thanks. It sucks, but this is life when you're dating a cop."

"I get it. Trust me. Finding Tony's killer is important, and you're on a clock. The pizza at Monkeypod can wait until next week. I'm not mad."

"Cool. Okay, I'll text you when things get less intense. Maybe we can grab a quick coffee or something later this week."

"I'd like that."

We walked back to the group, where Liam was continuing to pester Vesper, who was flipping him off while miming zipping her lips with her other hand.

"Okay, Liam, let's go," Jake said firmly. "Vesper, can you arrange with your lawyer to meet at the police station later? Here's my card. We just want to talk."

"Got it," Vesper said, taking the business card Jake handed her. "I'm not saying a word until then."

"Understood," Jake said. He nodded at us then turned and left, half dragging Liam behind him.

"What did the two of you talk about?" Zoe asked.

"He wants me to know that they don't automatically suspect Vesper and that he wants to find the real killer, but that just because she lives in our building doesn't mean he can write her off as a suspect."

"I mean, I get that," Vesper said with a shrug. "I won't hold this against him unless he tries to actually put me in jail."

"He also said you were suspected of doing a few things back in the eighties."

"I was never charged," Vesper replied with mischievous smirk. "Besides, that was a long time ago. I'm too old to do anything illegal anymore. It's one thing to run from the cops when you're twenty-five. It's another at fifty-five. I just don't have the energy. I want to sit at home, drink my wine, and go out surfing with my friends from time to time. And I guess I have to show up to work occasionally too."

I laughed. "Sounds like a life."

"Exactly. And I enjoy my life. So Jake better not try and put me in jail for this, because I didn't do it. And that partner of his, Liam, is an idiot. I don't trust him one bit."

"Me either," I muttered. "So what's going to

happen with the competition? I assume it'll be cancelled."

"For today, absolutely. The organizers will decide what's going to happen. They might delay it a few days or a week if they can, or they might just decide that's too much work and cancel it until next year. We'll see. But with the whole area being an active crime scene, and given what happened to Tony, there's no way they'll hold it on schedule," Vesper said.

"What's going to happen to the raffle?" I asked.

"Charlie," Zoe scolded.

"What? It's a valid question."

"A man's been murdered."

"Yes, and that's very sad, but there are real-life considerations and questions that still need to be asked."

"You could wait more than thirty minutes after he died to ask them."

"Let me guess—Charlie has entered this competition because she saw the raffle prize for free pie," Vesper said with a cackle.

"Am I *that* predictable?"

"Well, given as you once told me that the ocean is full of pervert dolphins and whales that try to eat you, I had to assume it wasn't your newfound love for this sport that got you on the water."

"I guess that's fair," I admitted.

"I already told you the pervert dolphins thing isn't real," Zoe said.

"The internet said it is, and would the internet lie to me?"

"Yes. One hundred trillion percent yes. The internet is *full* of lies and misinformation."

"The internet also told me if I was a potato, I would be a tater tot, and I agree with that."

"No, you would be a baked potato because you're full of hot air and ranch dressing, and you love bacon."

"Hey, that's way better than what that quiz said," I said.

"And we're getting off topic. Vesper, you are completely right. Charlie is here for her chance to win the pie."

"Whatever gets you out on the water. I imagine the raffle will only happen if we can solve this case."

"Okay, I'm going to go talk to some people and see what else I can find out about Tony," I said. "We need to solve this. We have to clear your name, and the sooner this case is solved, the more likely the competition is to go ahead, since the sponsors won't have that mystery hanging over them."

"I'll hang out with you. You don't know anybody here, but I do. These are my people," Vesper replied.

"Thanks. Zoe, the car keys are in my bag that I left on the beach over there."

"I'm good. Henry is coming over in a few minutes anyway. He was planning on coming to see us."

I wiggled my eyebrows. "He was coming to see you, huh?"

"Yes. Because I invited my new boyfriend to come to this event that's important to me, because I'm a normal human being who understands how relationships work," she said pointedly. "You should have invited Jake."

"He's here, isn't he?"

"This does not count."

"It should. Anyway, have fun with Henry."

"Thanks. Someone brought your board in; I saw it on the beach over there. Are you good if I leave them both in the back of Queenie?"

"Yeah, no problem. I'll bring them home."

"Cool."

With that, Zoe waved and headed off.

I turned to Vesper. "All right. Let's go find a murderer."

Chapter 6

"Who do you want to talk to first?" Vesper asked.

"The business partner, Daniel Yang. I think that's a good place to start, since he's an obvious suspect. And if he didn't do it, he might know who did. I also want to talk to the girlfriend, Lily, but with the EMTs around and given that she's probably in shock, I think it would be best to wait a bit."

Vesper nodded. "Sounds good. Come on."

Vesper led me to the group of people Daniel was speaking with.

"Vesper," Daniel immediately said when he saw her. He opened his arms wide and gave her a quick hug. "How are you holding up? It's such awful news, isn't it?"

"They think I killed him, Daniel," Vesper replied, her voice trembling slightly. I had a sneaking suspicion she was putting on a bit of a show; she hadn't been like this at all when we spoke to her.

"You're joking," he said, shaking his head.

"That's bull," said one of the men Daniel had been talking to. "Total bull. Anyone who knows you, Vesper, knows you wouldn't kill anyone."

"Or if you did, you'd at least do it well enough to not get caught," the other man said.

"Thank you," Vesper replied. "I agree completely. But you know what the cops are like. Always look at the ex. So this is Charlie, a friend of mine who's a private investigator. She's going to look into this and clear my name, and she was hoping to ask Daniel here a few questions about Tony. Just getting the lay of the land with what things were like with him, you know?"

"Cool, we'll leave you to it," said the first of the two men who had been speaking to Daniel. "Talk to you later. Good luck with everything. I hope you find who killed Tony. He was a good guy."

"I'll do my best," I replied.

They walked off, and Daniel held out a hand, which I took. His grip was firm without being overly tight, and he looked me in the eye as he introduced himself. "Daniel Yang. It's nice to meet you, although not under these circumstances."

"Charlie Gibson. I'm sorry for your loss."

"Thank you. How can I help?"

"As Vesper says, I'm just gathering information right now. I'm trying to figure out who Tony was, what his life was like, and who might have wanted him dead. Vesper says you knew him better than anyone."

"I sure do. Did. Wow, it's weird just phrasing it like that, you know? I grew up on Oahu and met Tony on the surfing circuit when we were teenagers. Vesper too. He was three years older than me, and as a fourteen-year-old, seeing someone like Tony who could ride a board like he did was unbelievable. I really looked up to him. Eventually, I retired from pro surfing and tried getting a real job. I was an accountant for a while."

"There's no way I ever would have trusted you with my taxes," Vesper teased.

Daniel laughed good-naturedly. "No, I don't know why anyone ever did. It didn't take long for me to realize accounting wasn't my calling. Or even something I could pretend to be good at to make a living. I quit my job, and my boyfriend dumped me for it. I was heartbroken at the time, but it turned out to be an opportunity. I packed up and moved to Maui, thinking maybe another island would be a fresh start.

"Tony reached out, said he'd heard I'd just moved to the island, and that he was thinking of starting a new company. Asked if I wanted in, told me he knew how to build a mean board but needed someone who could manage the business side of things. I warned him that I was the world's shittiest accountant but that I'd do my best. He said that was fine."

I raised my eyebrows. "That didn't throw up any red flags?"

Daniel shrugged. "I was someone from the same world as Tony. I knew him and had for decades at this point, even if we weren't best friends. That kind of bond, that kind of relationship, knowing someone from the surfing world like that, it's worth more than a fancy MBA from one of those business schools on the mainland. Surfing is more than just an industry. It's a lifestyle, and Tony knew that better than anyone."

Vesper nodded. "Daniel's right. Having him on board as one of the partners would have meant more credibility in the surfing world. Daniel Yang was a big name in surfing once upon a time."

"Hey, I can still hold my own on a board," Daniel replied with a grin.

"And that's why you were the right choice as a business partner."

"Exactly. So Tony and I founded Sharky Surfboards."

"Sharky?" I asked.

"Named after Jaws, the wave out here. We started making custom boards for people. Initially, we were Maui-only. We figured start small, you know? But Tony, he was great at sales, I got to give him that. Plus between us, we knew basically every serious surfer on the island already, so we signed a few up-and-comers to pro deals, we got the word out, and next thing you know, everyone is after a Sharky."

"Congratulations," I said. "It's not easy starting a new business."

"No, it's not. But Tony was great to work with. He got along with everyone, and he knew everyone. He was the kind of guy who could work a room, so we had no problems raising that initial capital, letting everyone know we were an option, and building sales. Plus Tony's boards were great. He knew what he was doing."

Vesper added, "He was right into it, ever since we were kids. I remember when we were teenagers, the idea of building boards always appealed to Tony. He didn't have any of the equipment to do it at the time, of course, but he'd find an old plank of wood and try and use his dad's tools to turn it into a board, then he'd take it out on the water."

Daniel laughed. "Yeah, that sounds like him."

"Did it work?" I asked.

"Let me put it this way: most of the time, it was like asking a guy who's used to driving a Ferrari to take out his grandpa's old Buick and drive it around the track at Monaco," Vesper said. "It was terrible, but Tony thought it was a hoot. I wasn't the least bit surprised when I heard he was opening his own board shop."

"So business was good? How long ago did you and Tony start working together?"

Daniel pursed his lips as he thought about the answer. "Must have been twelve, thirteen years ago now. Something like that. Geez, time passes quickly. Feels like yesterday sometimes. But yes, business was good. We ship our boards worldwide now. We have a whole network of companies we work with to distribute. We went from being a dinky little company working in a shed behind Tony's home to having a whole warehouse and factory set up here on the outskirts of Paia. I know you're going to look into Sharky, because you have to, but there was nothing going on in the business. We made money. We made a decent living. We have a handful of employees now, but there hasn't been any trouble with them at all."

"Are you primarily the one who deals with them, or was it Tony's role?" I asked.

"A bit of both, depending on their specific jobs. I handle the back-of-house stuff, so anyone who works in administration is under my purview, whereas Tony managed everyone in the workshop. The sales staff was a joint effort. Tony was the public face of the company, so he would work with them a lot, but they also did quite a bit in the office these days with me. But as I said, there haven't been problems with anyone."

"Okay," I said, nodding. "What about Tony's personal life?"

Daniel glanced over at Vesper quickly, and she held up her hands. "I know when to make myself scarce. I'm gone. Don't you worry about me."

Vesper scurried off, and Daniel turned to me. "Lily was the love of his life."

"Look, I know he was your best friend and he just passed away, but this is a murder investigation. And I heard from Vesper that Tony was a bit of a ladies' man."

"He was that. Yes, Tony loved the ladies. But I think it was more than that. I think Tony, ultimately, was afraid of being alone. He didn't know how to do it. He was like a child in some respects, always needing someone near him. I didn't think it was healthy if I'm honest with you. But then, I'm a gay man who grew up in the eighties. I lost a lot of friends to sleeping around. And I know it's different now, health-wise—and was never that different for straight people—but I still don't think it was healthy, mentally. Tony was a great guy who attracted women, and I understand why he did. But he never respected them enough to be monogamous.

"I'll be honest with you: I was surprised when I found out he was dating Vesper. I thought she had more sense than that. She knew the kind of guy that he was; she'd known him for decades. But she didn't seem to care. Tony was always Tony. He had a wandering eye, and he wasn't the kind to settle down. Not until Lily, anyway."

"He wasn't cheating on her?"

"No. And it's one of the things that made me realize they would be together forever. I never thought Tony would find someone to be with monogamously. I thought he would be a playboy forever. Then he met Lily."

"Can you tell me about that?"

Daniel tilted his head. "You can't think she would have anything to do with this."

"I don't," I said quickly. "I'm just trying to learn everything I can about Tony. About his life and the people in it. I genuinely don't suspect anybody at the moment. It's way too early for that."

Satisfied, Daniel nodded. "Good. I don't want her to be unfairly caught up in this. I know Vesper will be, what with their history, and that's unfair too. But Vesper can handle it. She's strong, mentally and physically. I once saw her tell a douchebag who was harassing her in a restaurant that she was going to steal his girlfriend and make her forget he ever existed. When the guy said there was no way she could compete with what he was packing, Vesper pointed to her prosthetic leg and said she had more to offer than he could ever compete with. The guy went white and left her alone after that."

I burst out laughing. "Yeah, that sounds like Vesper."

"But Lily, she's not like that. She's the opposite. She's quiet, reserved."

"How did she and Tony meet, and when?"

"It was in the hospital, I think. About, I don't know, maybe ten months ago? Tony was there for his dialysis. Lily was undergoing some sort of test. I'm not sure what, and it isn't my place to ask or to go around telling other people, anyway. You'd have to ask her. They ended up chatting, and the two hit it off immediately."

"So they started dating right then and there?"

Daniel frowned. "Well, this is where it gets tricky. Tony was still with Vesper then, so he couldn't admit publicly that they were going out straight away. I'm not sure they did, either. They were just getting to know each other. I'm not actually sure he told Lily about Vesper to begin with, either. That was the thing about Tony—he was a coward. He would wait until the women found out he was cheating and dump him rather than actually being honest with them and tell him he'd found someone else. I think that was part of the fun for him, really. The living two lives."

"That's really fucked up."

"I know. You won't find any disagreement here. Tony was a great friend of mine, and I'm heartbroken he's gone, but I won't pretend he was an angel. His personal life was a mess."

"Okay. So eventually, Vesper finds out about Lily and breaks up with him."

"Yeah. And honestly, I think Tony was more in love with Vesper than he realized. When she dumped him, he was more broken up than I'd ever seen him before. Then I found out from Vesper that he was stalking her. But apparently, that stopped pretty quickly."

"Vesper said she'd drop a match into his gas tank if he kept parking at our apartment building."

"I'm glad he got the message. Anyway, he publicly started dating Lily *very* soon after that. But he was different. There was no more looking at other women. No more flirting with anyone who came into the office with a pair of boobs. He honestly seemed like a changed man."

I raised my eyebrows. "What was it about Lily that he liked so much?"

"I asked him once. He said she had a different vibe from everyone else he had ever dated. She was more mature."

"I would hope so, given the age difference," I said dryly.

"Yes, it's a bit of a red flag, isn't it?" Daniel agreed. "Lily is twenty-six, so there's a good twenty-five years between them. But they're consenting adults. And it has been the most stable relationship

Tony has been in since I've known him. Maybe ever."

"Tell me about the kidney transplant."

"Well, Tony was on the list, but he was probably a few years out still. Shortly after they met, Lily suggested she get herself tested and see if she would be a good match. Tony didn't want her to. Said it wasn't on her to do something like that and that he didn't want her to risk giving up some of her life for his, but she insisted. We all knew the odds of them being a match were tiny, but it came up almost perfect."

"That's very lucky for Tony."

"Exactly. Tony didn't want Lily to give up a kidney, but we managed to convince him it was the best thing for him. After all, Tony had been going downhill, health wise, the past few years. There were no guarantees he was going to make it until he got to the top of the transplant list. If Lily was willing to do this for him, he should accept."

"And eventually, he did."

"Yeah. It took some convincing, but he agreed. They went through the whole process, and Tony finally got his new kidney. It was incredible seeing the change in him. It was like he was a new man. And of course, Lily was amazing. She went through that kind of invasive surgery, and she came out of it like a champ. Of course, they weren't allowed to do any real exercise for six weeks, and they had to stay out of the water for a bit longer, but eventually, the doctors cleared them both to go back to leading regular lives. But they're not allowed to do kick-boxing or anything else that might damage the kidneys."

"But surfing is fine?" I asked, my eyebrows rising.

"I think the doctors understood that even if it wasn't, Tony wasn't willing to give it up and would just do it anyway. He was told to be careful."

"Does Lily surf?"

"She got into it a bit after she started dating Tony. She's a quick learner, and I've been very impressed by her. But of course, Tony also has decades of experience teaching kids at this point too. He taught her himself. She'll never be a pro, of course, but she's a decent intermediate-level boarder."

"And they were both competing here today?"

"Yeah. It was going to be Lily's first-ever competition. They were doing it as a couple. It was supposed to be such a fun time for them."

"Okay. And there weren't any problems that you know of between them after the transplant?"

"No. Not at all. Like I said, Tony seemed like a changed man. And honestly, if I had seen anything that even hinted that he was cheating on Lily, I would have told him to pull his head in. She gave him a kidney, for God's sake. I know that doesn't give you the right to own a person forever, but at the very least, he owed it to her to be honest with her. So knowing his history, I kept an eye out, but there were no signs at all. He wasn't cheating. I wouldn't have been surprised if for the first time in his life, he was thinking about marriage."

I nodded. "Okay. What about Vesper now that she's left? She's obviously one of the main suspects here."

"Yes. As soon as I heard it was murder, I knew she would be. Vesper is known to have a bit of a wild streak to her. And everyone in the surfing community knows about their messy breakup. It wasn't that long ago. And for Tony to then turn around and get a kidney from the woman we all know he was cheating on Vesper with? It's kind of a given to hone in on her as the prime suspect."

"Do you think she could have done it?"

"Well, that's the thing. All of that said, I don't think she would have. Maybe I'm just being naïve and want to believe the best in people. But I don't see Vesper as being a killer. I don't think she did this. But I also can't imagine who would have."

"I heard Tony ran a program here to teach kids how to surf."

"Yeah, that was his pride and joy. It's a program aimed at local *keiki*, especially those whose parents can't afford lessons. Once a week, Tony would take them out onto the water, along with a few other instructors, and he'd teach them how to surf. Tony supplied the surfboards. A lot he made himself in his spare time, but he also used his networks to get anyone with an old board they were trying to get rid of to sell it to him for cheap or free. He'd let the kids use the boards for as long as they wanted."

"That's great."

"I agree. It was a fantastic program and an amazing opportunity for local children. He's taught hundreds of kids on this island how to surf. I know Tony wasn't perfect, but he was a good person. He did a lot for Maui and for the surfing community."

I nodded. "I'm going to do what I can to find his killer. Can you point me in any direction that could help?"

I received a blank look in reply. "I wish I could. I really do. But I knew Tony better than anyone, and I don't think... actually, you know what?"

"Yeah?"

"I just remembered, I think there was something going on between him and one of the guys on the factory floor."

"Oh?"

"Look, it's probably nothing. I don't think there was even an issue between them. But for a couple of weeks, Tony has been spending a lot of time with one of the workers in the factory—Andrew. I don't know if he's mentoring him or training him up to do something else or what. I asked about it once, and Tony said it was nothing, he just needed some extra guidance."

"But you think there was more to it than that?" I asked.

"It could be. I mean, I can't be sure. But I've known Tony a long time."

I nodded. "Can I come by the factory sometime and talk to Andrew?"

"Sure. It's Saturday, so we'll be open on Monday. I don't know if we'll do much other than remember Tony, but I think the staff will want the opportunity to come in and pay their respects. I know I'll be there. You're welcome to stop by."

"Thanks. I appreciate the help."

"If I can think of anything else, I'll let you know. But I'm telling you, everyone loved Tony. Well, apart from his exes. But Vesper is the only one of them who was on the water today."

"Are there any others here today? Anyone else I could talk to?"

"Uh, sure," Daniel said, his eyes scanning the crowd. "Over there at the table, see the brunette at the computer, talking to Leslie?"

"Yeah, I do." Leslie was my boss at Aloha Ice Cream, the primary sponsor of this event.

"That's Joy Hargraves. She was with Tony about a year and a half, maybe two years ago. Before Vesper, anyway. You could see what she has to say."

"Great. Thanks," I said.

"Good luck. I do hope you find who did this. Tony was a good guy, and I'm going to miss him."

"I'll do my best."

I headed down the beach, thinking over what I'd just heard. Professionally, Tony seemed to have his ducks mostly in a row, although I wanted to talk to Andrew. His personal life had been a dumpster fire, but had he really put all of that behind him and turned over a new leaf? And if so, did that mean a ghost from his past had come back to haunt him? I was going to have to find out.

Chapter 7

I was walking toward the picnic tables when Leslie spotted me and waved. I waved back and headed toward her, where she was speaking with Joy Hargraves.

"I know you signed up, but I still wasn't sure you were actually going to do it," Leslie said, a twinkle in her eye. She was an avid surfer and had been friends with Vesper for years. I only worked about a shift a week at Aloha Ice Cream these days, with my private investigation business taking up most of my time, and I was grateful to Leslie for letting me essentially pick my own schedule.

"You know my motivation," I replied with a wink. "But of course, I assume the competition has been cancelled."

"Yes. It's awful, really. Poor Tony. I can't believe

something like that would happen here. I heard he was stabbed."

I nodded. "Yes. Zoe and I found the body. Someone stabbed him in the back."

Joy shuddered. She looked to be in her mid-, maybe late forties, with a light tan and caramel-colored hair streaked with blond. Her waves hung just past her shoulders, and she looked at me with big, round eyes and a friendly face. "You must be Charlie. Leslie has told me a lot about you. I'm Joy."

"It's very nice to meet you," I replied. "In fact, I actually came here to talk to you, Joy. Daniel Yang sent me over, he told me you might be able to help. I'm trying to solve Tony's murder, since Vesper is one of the main suspects."

Joy scowled. "Yeah, I bet. Always look at the jilted woman. Not whether the idiot victim was asking for it."

"Joy," Leslie said, warning in her tone. "Charlie is cool, but be careful who you're talking like that to. Tony had a lot of friends around here."

"That's because men will put their own friend-ships in front of knowing a guy is a total twatwaffle and calling him out on it," Joy replied. "Seriously, if any of us tried half the stuff Tony did, we would have been ostracized in a minute by those guys."

"I get it, but Tony's been murdered, and they're going to look at his exes," Leslie said. She looked up at me. "Since you're involved, that means they've already spoken to Vesper. I saw the cops. Jake is one of them, isn't he?"

I nodded. "Yeah. Which is good. He's going to try and get to the truth. He won't just lock up the first person who looks like they might have done it."

"You might trust him, but I don't," Joy said.

"Then trust me. I'm friends with Vesper. Leslie can vouch for me too. I'm going to do my best to catch the killer."

Leslie nodded. "You can be honest with Charlie, Joy. But for the love of your freedom, please stop mentioning how much of an asshole Tony was in front of other people. Especially if the cops make it here."

"Okay. What do you want to know? I will tell you everything, because you're not going to get it from the men he was friends with. You just finished speaking to Daniel?"

"That's right," I replied.

"I don't know what Daniel told you, but Tony was a dick. I get it. I'm the jilted ex. And I should have known better going into that relationship. But here's the thing. It wasn't just the cheating. I did delude myself into thinking I'd be the woman who would change him, who would finally make him see the error of his ways. And that was stupid of me. But whatever. I signed up for that part of it, and I know it was a mistake. What I didn't sign up for was his mood swings and temper."

"Was he abusive?" I asked.

"Borderline. He never actually hit me. But he would get angry if I stayed out too late. He'd throw things at the wall. Never in front of other people, though. Always in private. He'd apologize after, of course. It felt like abuse sometimes. But I loved him, and my dumb ass stayed. Until I found out he was seeing someone else at the same time. That was it. I knew it was over, and I wasn't going to stick around until he dragged me into the depths of hell. Don't get me wrong. I was not totally innocent in this, but Tony Murray treated women like playthings that existed solely for his own enjoyment, and I am not surprised that it eventually caught up to him."

Leslie nodded. "He's always had a bad reputation."

"But he gets along so well with everyone in public, so he gaslights you into thinking you're the problem. And the rest of the world believes it too," Joy said. "I'd tell people what he did, and they'd go 'Oh, Tony? Really? No, he's not like that. It can't be true.' And yet he was. I didn't kill him, but I'm not sad he's dead."

"Do you know who might have wanted him dead?"

"I'd look at whoever he's dating now. Or anyone

he dated in the past. Or anyone he was otherwise close to."

"Like Daniel?"

"Exactly like Daniel."

"I just finished speaking to him. He had nothing bad to say about Tony at all."

"Yeah, because he's better than Joy at hiding his real feelings about the guy," Leslie said with a snort. "I'm sure overall, they got along, but running a business together is a real relationship. Believe me, I know; I started Aloha Ice Cream with my ex-husband."

"Well, if there was trouble at the company, he pretended it didn't exist."

"That doesn't surprise me. But I bet it was there. Tony was great on the surface. It was once you got to know him that he became more difficult to deal with. But his true betrayal, he kept for women. He didn't respect us at all. Whereas Daniel, at least, was a man."

"What do you think of Lily?"

Joy shrugged. "When they first got together, I thought she was a naïve little girl who was going to be chewed up and spit out by Tony the instant his roaming eyes landed on something just a little bit different. I felt sorry for her. She wasn't from the surfing world. She didn't know who Tony was. At least I had that foreknowledge. I went in with my eyes wide open. I was just an idiot for doing it anyway. But Lily? No, she didn't have a clue, and I felt bad about it.

"But in the end, what did I know? She gave him her kidney, and I thought it was the worst decision in the world. I went and saw her, you know? After I found out what she was doing. I wanted to warn her. But she told me she knew what she was doing, and it was her choice to make."

"And she went ahead and did it anyway. But from what I've seen, the two were serious," I said.

"That's what it looked like, but a leopard doesn't change its spots. I don't care how well it's pretending. I know everyone thinks Tony was a changed man and that he was finally going to settle down with Lily. Maybe even propose to her. But I know the truth. There wasn't a chance in hell. Tony was doing the right thing because after taking her kidney, he knew even he wasn't going to get away with dumping her like he did all of us and still be able to maintain his reputation in the community. Men will turn a blind eye to what other men do on a lot of occasions, but there's a limit. And cheating on then dumping the woman who gave you a kidney is near the top of that list."

"So you didn't believe it was going to last."

"Nope. But Tony has everyone under his thumb, and they all believe it. That's the worst part, you know? When you've realized the truth about someone, but nobody else sees it. You feel like you're going insane. But I guarantee you, it was going to go bad between them. It just hadn't yet."

I nodded. "What do you think of Lily now?"

"I feel bad for her," Joy admitted.

"You're not jealous? No resentment at all?"

"No. She's a young little thing. Around your age. She doesn't know Tony. They met in the hospital; she was there for her cousin, I think. I consider her to be another one of his victims. I'm just glad for her that he died before he really betrayed her and broke her heart. It's too bad whoever killed him didn't think to do it before he got the kidney off her."

"So you don't think Lily killed him?"

"Not a chance. She loved him. It was obvious to anyone who saw them together."

"I saw them arrive," Leslie chimed in. "While I was setting up the ice cream stand to sell from. They certainly looked like a couple in love. Lily had that adoring look in her eye that only comes from youth."

Joy chuckled. "Sounds right. It's been that way every time I saw them together too. No, Charlie, when it comes to this sort of thing, I believe women. Because I know how often we're manipulated into thinking other women are the enemy when they're not. As a gender, we're more powerful when we stick together. So I don't resent Lily at all, even though Tony is my ex. I was on her side, and I was hoping she would see the light. She didn't, but someone else had obviously had enough of him."

"This is where I'm running into problems, though," I admitted. "The only people who seemed to take issue with Tony were the women who dated him. We have Vesper, and we have you, Kamalani, and who else? Surely the women he dated before you have moved on with their lives. They would have killed him long ago, wouldn't they?"

"That is true," Joy admitted. "Well, if he was killed on the water, it wasn't me who did it. I was up here the whole time. I'm working behind the scenes in data. I get the scores from the judges and plug them into the computer to find out who won. I don't have time to go out to catch a few waves today."

"And I can confirm that. I was over there at the Aloha Ice Cream truck with Samantha, getting everything ready. Every time I looked over, Joy was here at the computer," Leslie said.

"Okay. So you didn't do it, Vesper didn't do it, and Lily didn't do it. Who did?"

"Dig into his life. And I don't mean his public life, the one other surfers know about," Joy suggested. "If Tony was cheating on all of us, he had more than just one side piece going at a time. I guarantee it. Men like that, they only admit to the ones they're caught with. There were more women. I doubt any of them were recent—even he would have known better than that so soon after the surgery—but they're out there. And some of them might not have taken it well when Tony dumped them."

I nodded. "Right. Thanks for the advice."

Vesper sidled up next to me then. "Found some of my favorite people, have you?" she asked. "Let me guess: Joy is telling you what a big fan of Tony she was."

Leslie laughed. "Yeah, that's right."

"Joy here did warn me," Vesper said.

"Well, we both made the same dumb mistake. What can I say? We were young."

"Honey, we were in our late forties," Vesper replied with a cackling laugh.

"I'm still young at heart, and that's the important thing."

"That's true," I said. "Can you tell me where Tony lived?"

"Yeah, I'll text you the address," Vesper said.

"Thanks. I'll have to wait a bit. The police will want to check it out first, and it's probably not a great idea to be in the house at the same time as them."

"Right."

"I think I have enough to go on for now. I'm going to see a couple of friends and find out what we can uncover about Tony."

"Good luck," Leslie said.

"If it weren't for the fact that Vesper and I are

probably suspects, I'd tell you I hope whoever did this gets away with it," Joy said. "But I like my freedom more than I wanted Tony dead, so I do hope you get to the bottom of this."

"Me too," Vesper agreed.

"I will do my best. By the way, I highly recommend not talking to the cops without a lawyer. And you can tell them Charlie told you that."

I walked back toward Queenie, deep in thought. I had learned a lot about Tony's life, and it seemed, for now, that he had been the kind of person who would have a lot of secrets. I had to see Dot and Rosie.

Chapter 8

I hopped into the driver's seat and sent off a text to our group chat.

I have a new client. Vesper, my neighbor. She's the prime suspect in the murder of her ex-boyfriend, who appears to have been quite the womanizer. I bet his digital footprint is going to be a disaster. Do you both want in?

Nothing makes me happier than looking into someone's personal life that's messier than a daycare center on finger painting day, Dot replied a minute later.

Cool. I'll be there in about an hour. I'm leaving now, but I have to drop our surfboards back at our place.

Does this mean you didn't win the free pie? Dot asked.

There's no raffle if there's no competition. Unsure as to what's happening on that front yet. So, no pie.

That's the worst news I've heard all day.

A man was murdered, Rosie pointed out.

It doesn't sound like he was a particularly good guy,

though. And let's be honest, there's a certain bar to clear if you want to be considered better than free pie.

I laughed, turned on the Jeep, and slowly drove back out to the road and the highway that would take me home.

A little over an hour later, I was knocking on Dot's door at her apartment building, and it swung open to reveal Rosie.

"Two whole weeks without a murder in this town. Who was it this time?" she asked as I entered.

"Tony Murray. Apparently, he's well known in surfing circles."

"Oh, I've heard of him," Rosie said with a nod. "He was a pro back in the eighties and nineties, wasn't he? Now he runs that camp for local kids to teach them how to surf."

"That's the one. This morning, while everyone was warming up, someone decided to stick a knife in his back."

"No kidding," Dot said. "I heard from a friend that something was going on up north, but I didn't have details."

"Zoe and I found the body. The competition has been postponed at the very least—hence the lack of pie—but Vesper is one of the main suspects. They're looking at his exes, and she's the most recent one that's publicly known about. But another woman, another ex, said to dig deeper into his personal life. She suspects there are more women out there who would have had reasons to want him dead, and I suspect she's right."

"And in this day and age of technology, the easiest way to find people to hook up with is the internet," Rosie said, nodding.

"Good. I've been bored out of my mind. Ever since that Jordan Sumner headed back to Seattle without trying anything, I feel like I haven't had anything to do."

An involuntary shiver ran down my spine at the name. Jordan Sumner had links with the Ham brothers back in Seattle. I had killed their brother, Stevie, when he'd tried to rob the store I worked at, and that was the reason I'd come back to Hawaii in the first place. Just before Christmas, I had found out they knew where I lived now.

We had followed Jordan Sumner, thinking that he was going to try and find me, but he spent a few days relaxing on the beach in Wailoa then flew back to Seattle. It could have been a coincidence, a vacation that just so happened to coincide with where I was now living, but I didn't believe that. And neither did Dot and Rosie. We were keeping track of the Ham brothers and their Seattle crew, and if they tried anything, we would be ready.

"Oh, come on," Rosie said. "You spent all of last week at that computer, exposing that NFT site as being a scam, and you brought the whole company down."

"Well, it was a scam. The owner was funneling all the money to offshore accounts, where it couldn't be traced, and the so-called NFTs were just jpeg images."

"Still, it wasn't boring."

"No. But I was bored *today*. So I'm glad Charlie brought us this case. You say he was a womanizer?"

I nodded and ran the two women through everything I'd learned about Tony that morning.

"I hate people like that," Dot said when I was finished. "My ex was the same way. Everyone thought he was the greatest guy. But they didn't see what he said to me when we were alone, behind closed doors. It made me terrified to leave him. I thought if I did, I'd be seen as the bad one. And I was, by a lot of people."

"This is going to be big news for the island," Rosie mused. "There will be pressure to get the case solved. And you said Jake is on it?"

"Yes. And Liam, which is much worse. But I know Jake will do right by Vesper. If she didn't kill Tony, he's not going to go after her."

"All the same, it would be best for us to quickly find the real killer."

"Great," Dot said. "Let's do it. First things first: we have to find his secondary phone number. And his dating site profiles."

"Would he use them?" I asked. "After all, it would be pretty easy for the women he's seeing to find those, wouldn't it? All it takes is a friend scrolling who happens to come across it, and it's all over."

Dot shook her head. "No. Men like that, serial cheaters, they know what they're doing. They'll have the profiles set up so that there's no way they'll come across their current partner's friends, or they'll just pretend that it's an old account they haven't used in years. We just have to find it."

"Okay, so we do what? Hack into the company's servers?"

"Well, the easiest thing to do would be to get access to the phone Tony used the app with."

I shook my head. "Not until the police are done going through his place. That's the end of the day, at least."

"Who's got time to wait for that? We're going to do this the old-fashioned way: create a profile on all the big dating apps and try to find Tony's profile through brute force. Once we have it, I can hack into his account and see who he's been talking to, but we need a username for him first," Dot said. "I'll take Tinder. Rosie, you download Thirsty."

"Thirsty? Is that the name of the app? That's a terrible name for a dating app."

I snickered. "I guess that particular slang hasn't made it to your gen—I mean, to this specific part of the island. Someone who's thirsty is said to really want attention, especially sexually."

"I suppose that makes sense, and nice save," Rosie said. "All right, I'll download the app. Who are we pretending to be?"

"If his current girlfriend is in her twenties, we'll go older. From what we've learned from Charlie, Tony didn't seem to be the type to always go for the younger girls. And he may have raised his minimum age limit to prevent any of Lily's friends from coming across his profile and having to answer unwanted questions, as Charlie said. Let's say thirty-five."

"Got it," Rosie said.

"And Charlie, you take the Tinder."

"Yeah, I know it well," I said dryly.

"You're taken these days, aren't you?" Rosie said with a sly smile. "Don't tell me you're taking after Tony Murray."

I laughed. "No. I just have a long list of mostly disastrous meetups from before I moved here. I eventually realized I wasn't made for online dating. Not when I seem to attract every single weirdo within a ten-mile radius of me."

I opened up my app, logged out, and then began the process of signing up again. I downloaded a couple pictures from Google Images and uploaded them as my profile pictures, and soon, I was in.

I was no longer Charlie Gibson, the sexy private investigator with a great sense of humor. I was now

Carly Fremont, an even sexier schoolteacher whose interests included surfing, was looking for someone a bit older, and otherwise had absolutely no personality, because I figured keeping everything else wide open would make it more likely that we would find Tony Murray's profile faster.

As soon as my account was ready, I started scrolling through profile photos, swiping left on all of them.

"I swear, a guy posing with a surfboard is the Hawaii equivalent of a guy holding up a fish he caught back on the mainland," I said after a couple of minutes.

"I just saw one who took a selfie in his truck with a hat and sunglasses, doing the shaka with one hand," Rosie said.

"This guy has a whole list of things he doesn't want in a woman," Dot said. "No tattoos. No colored hair. Natural body parts only."

"I guess Vesper's out," I said with a grin.

"Oh boy, this list gets worse."

"That list already has more red flags than a Communist Party rally. How can it *possibly* get worse?" Rosie asked.

Dot continued reading. "Must have a BMI of under nineteen. Laziness is unattractive."

"Isn't nineteen underweight?" I asked.

"Apparently, eating food is considered lazy," Dot said. "Also, no one who uses pronouns."

I rolled my eyes.

"No one who wants to raise minimum wage."

"Ah, yes, this guy sounds like he cares about and knows a lot about the economy," Rosie said.

"No militant feminists. No one over five foot five."

"We need to get everyone on this app under that into a pair of heels, stat," I said.

"No one argumentative, and someone who understands that I know what's best for both of us."

Rosie made a gagging motion.

"And finally, no Nirvana fans."

"Well, that's the biggest deal breaker of them all right there," I said, laughing.

"No Nirvana fans? Why not? What did Kurt Cobain ever do to him?" Rosie asked.

Dot shrugged. "I have no idea, and I'm not about to message him to ask."

"The guy who doesn't want women with tattoos or fake boobs should love a band with a song titled "Come as You Are," I pointed out.

"Critical-thinking skills don't seem to be this man's strong suit," Rosie pointed out.

"And who is this fine specimen of the human race?" I asked with a grin.

"His name is Derek, and he lives within three miles of here."

"That's not nearly enough distance between us," Rosie said with a disgusted grimace.

"I feel like I should let Jake know I appreciate him, because wow," I said, shaking my head.

"This is why I never got married," Rosie announced. "Well, one of the reasons."

"And why I never should have," Dot said, shaking her head.

"Okay, well, if I ever see Derek, I'm going to accidentally run him over with Queenie just to do humanity a favor," I said.

Dot laughed and showed me the picture. "This is him."

I raised my eyebrows. Derek had a forehead you could land a jumbo jet on, stringy hair the color of a dirty puddle that reached down to his shoulders, and small, beady brown eyes. He was standing in front of a mirror in his bathroom that looked like it hadn't been cleaned this century, flexing nonexistent biceps.

"I'm shocked this guy still has a profile here, what with women obviously falling all over themselves to be with him," I said sarcastically, handing the phone to Dot.

"Let's get back on track. We're supposed to be looking for Tony's profile," Rosie said.

"Sometimes, you just have to take a moment to make fun of the true psychopaths on dating sites," I said with a grin.

"If you're doing that, we're going to be here forever."

"Most of them are better at hiding it than this guy, though," I said. "You don't always find out about the really weird stuff until you're on a date, and then you have to turn into a super spy, trying to figure out where the emergency exit is and how you can get out of there without him noticing."

"Hey, I found Tony," Rosie interrupted.

Dot and I immediately dropped our conversation and huddled around her. Sure enough, her app had a picture of Tony. He was standing on the beach, wearing board shorts, a rash guard, and a pair of Oakleys, smiling into the sun as he leaned casually against a surfboard.

"See, *this* is how you take a dating profile picture that doesn't make you look like you keep bodies in your basement freezer," I said. "That's definitely Tony."

"He's using his real name. And he's listed as being about fifteen miles away," Rosie said.

"That tracks, since he lives and works in Paia. No question it's him. Okay, Dot, what do you need to get into that account?"

Dot motioned for Rosie to hand her the phone. "Let me see that. An account number, some sort of identifier. There's bound to be one here somewhere, even if it's hidden in the underlying code. I'll find it."

Rosie gave her the phone, and Dot immediately

began typing away, moving to the main computer with its multiple monitors.

"Did you ever date?" I asked Rosie as I plonked myself on the couch, waiting for Dot to hack her way into the back end of the app and find all of the details of Tony's affairs.

"Once or twice," Rosie replied. "It was, of course, considered a little bit strange for a woman not to be married a few decades ago. I know tongues wagged. Some people must have imagined I was gay. It didn't bother me in the least, of course, but I did want to blend in as much as possible, so I would occasionally entertain a gentleman caller for a few hours."

"Meet anyone interesting?"

"No. They were all horribly boring. Invariably, they'd spend the entire date talking about themselves, as if the fact that they broke a friend's record playing *Space Invaders* or that they have a golf handicap of fourteen was ever actually going to impress me. Child, I knew snipers from the Second World War who killed fourteen Nazis. Your golf score is pathetic."

I laughed. "Yeah, that sounds about right."

"Eventually, I started a rumor that I was actually infertile, and that was the reason I wasn't settling down; I couldn't bring myself to get into a relationship with a man without being able to do what was, at the time, supposed to be the ultimate goal of a woman: bearing her man a child. After that, people stopped asking if I knew so-and-so and replaced those horrid conversations with looks of pity instead. It was certainly an improvement."

"I'm in," Dot announced then, and our conversation was interrupted as we went over to the computer.

"Okay, this is the back end of Tony's profile," Dot said as we approached.

Sure enough, there were Tony's pictures, all of the information from his profile, and a tab marked "private messages." Dot double-clicked on that one. On the left side of the screen was a list of women Tony had spoken to, and the rest was taken by the most recent conversation Tony had had on this app.

"This is dated from a year ago," I pointed out, noticing the time stamp. "Maybe everyone was right. Maybe Tony really had stopped using apps like these once he started dating Lily."

"It's possible," Dot said. "But read the messages. This woman isn't happy."

My eyes moved to the conversation between them. The text bubbles on the right were from Tony, the ones on the left from the woman. According to the bar on the right-hand side, her name was Chantelle.

I read from the top.

You're such an asshole, Tony. How could you do this to me?

You told me you loved me. I'm messaging you here because I've already blocked you on every single other social media site and changed my number. So don't bother contacting me anywhere else.

I do love you, Chantelle. The woman you saw me with, it's not what you think. She's my sister.

Oh, really? You have a sister with a prosthetic leg that you've never mentioned once before, when we've been dating for six months?

She likes her privacy. She's very sensitive about her leg.

I snorted when I read that line. For Halloween last year, Vesper had dressed up like a zombie baseball player, complete with Yankees outfit and hat, with the one pants leg rolled up, using her prosthetic as a bat. She sat outside our apartment in the yard, and the whole night, I knew when kids were coming our way from the screams.

No, Vesper was not sensitive about her leg, or lack thereof.

Do you really think I'm that dumb? Actually, you know what, don't answer that. You obviously do, since you didn't bother telling me I'm your fucking side piece. Have the life you deserve, you dick.

Beneath that, Tony had tried to message Chantelle back.

Look, I'm telling you, this is all a misunderstanding. You're being crazy, Chantelle. I love you. Can't you feel that from the way I've treated you? Let's talk about this.

Underneath, a message popped up. *The message*

you tried to send was undeliverable, as the recipient has blocked you.

"Good for her," I murmured.

Underneath, Tony had sent a whole bunch of other, abusive messages.

You dumb fucking bitch, I hope you die in a fire.

The message you tried to send was undeliverable, as the recipient has blocked you.

You're a fat whore who doesn't know what's good for her, and if I ever see you in the street, I'm going to punch you in the face so hard you lose two of the five teeth you have left, you dumb hick.

The message you tried to send was undeliverable, as the recipient has blocked you.

"Okay, Vesper was not lying when she said Tony had some anger issues," I said as I finished reading. "Tony did not handle being dumped well."

"We need to speak with Chantelle," Rosie said. "She's obviously smart; she preemptively blocked him, changed her phone number, and then contacted him on a single app she likely barely used before blocking him there as well. This isn't her first rodeo."

"I also wonder if Chantelle is the woman Vesper found out about," I mused. "After all, going by this, it sounds like he was dating them at the same time."

Dot scrolled up on the screen. "Their first inter-action was in November of last year. So it looks like

Tony and Chantelle were together for about four months."

"Yeah, that tracks with what Vesper said. She was with Tony for about eight, and she said it was his MO to find someone else after he got bored a few months in."

"He certainly has a temper, going by those messages he sent after he knew he was blocked," Rosie said, pursing her lips. "I don't like that at all."

"Me either," Dot said.

"It sounds like she hasn't spoken to Tony in a year, but I still want to talk to her," I said.

"Okay. I'll find you contact information for her, and Rosie and I will try and find Tony's profiles on other dating sites. If he was cheating on Lily, we'll find out about it."

"Cool. I'll come back here later. I think tonight, we should go check out his home. Late, after the police have gone."

"Sounds good."

Ten minutes later, Dot had hunted down a phone number for Chantelle for me. I hopped into Queenie and put the phone on speaker as I dialed the number.

Chapter 9

"Hello?" a voice answered on the other end of the line.

"Hi, is this Chantelle?"

"Yeah."

"I'm Charlie Gibson, a private investigator."

"And what do you want with me?" Her voice was tinged with a touch of snark, which I immediately appreciated.

"I have some news you probably won't mind hearing. Tony Murray, your ex, was murdered today."

"Huh. Go figure. And there's someone out there who actually gives enough of a shit about him to want the killer found, apart from the police?"

I had to give it to her, Chantelle was quick.

"Not exactly. I'm friends with another one of his

exes, and she's the prime suspect. She didn't do it, and I have to find out who did to clear her name."

"And you think it was me?"

"Not unless you were in the water at Ho'okipa this morning around seven. You're not a suspect, but I want to speak to you anyway. I'm trying to figure out who could have killed him."

"Sorry, can't help you. I do have an alibi; I was working. But as far as I'm concerned, whoever killed Tony probably did the world a favor, and I'm personally hoping they get away with it."

"That's not the first time I've heard that today, but if you don't help me, Vesper might go to jail for something she didn't do."

"Wait, Vesper? That's the ex that you're friends with? She's the prime suspect?"

"She sure is."

"Damn," Chantelle said quietly on the other end of the line. I didn't reply, and she spent a few seconds gathering her thoughts before continuing. "Okay, fine. I'll help you. I like Vesper. She doesn't deserve to go to jail. Where are you?"

"Kihei."

"I'm up in Lahaina."

"I can be there in thirty minutes."

I got the address from Chantelle then put Queenie into gear and pulled out of Dot's complex. It was time to see what Chantelle had for me.

LAHAINA WAS A CUTE TOWN, A FORMER FISHING village that was the capital of the Kingdom of Hawaii from 1820 to 1845 before the illegal annexation of the islands by the United States. Front Street, with its old-style restaurants and shops, was always packed full of tourists, and the harbor saw a constant stream of traffic, with everything from catamarans taking tourists out to snorkel to local fishermen dealing with the day's haul.

I drove past the enormous banyan tree that covered an entire acre, creating a miniature park in the center of town by itself—it had been planted back in 1873—and took one of the side roads toward the residential part of town where Chantelle lived.

Her home was a small bungalow, a very Hawaiian style, not unlike the one my mother lived in. It was painted a gorgeous robin's-egg blue, and the manicured lawn and plenty of native plants and flowers blooming all over made it immediately obvious that Chantelle had a green thumb.

I walked up to the front door and knocked, and she opened the door a moment later. Chantelle looked to be older than me, probably in her late thirties. Her blond hair obviously came from a bottle and was dotted with a few gray streaks here and there. Her light-blue eyes stood out from behind her slightly tanned skin, and she wore a tank top and cutoff denim shorts on her slim frame.

"You must be Charlie," she said when she saw me. She turned and left the door open for me to follow her into the house. "So Tony's really dead, huh? I didn't believe you when you told me, but I looked it up, and sure enough, some guy died on the north shore this morning. It was him?"

I nodded. "Yeah. I found the body myself. Stabbed in the back."

"Fitting way for him to go."

We entered an open living space, and Chantelle motioned for me to take a seat on the couch while she settled into an armchair on the other side of the living room, slowly rocking back and forth.

"How'd you find me?"

"One of his dating apps," I explained. "You were the last person Tony messaged."

Chantelle snorted. "Yeah, I doubt that. Tony wasn't the kind of guy who could be monogamous. I was an idiot for believing in him. But he was cheating on me with Vesper. If you saw the messages, you know what I sent him."

I nodded. "You saw the two of them together?"

"Yeah. Total fluke, too. I had an appointment with my optometrist. I was going down South Kihei Road, stuck in traffic, of course, and I saw the two of them on Kam One, arm in arm, watching the sunset. I stopped just to be sure, but it was definitely him."

"What did you do then?"

"Went to my appointment, then blocked him on all social media. I changed my phone number, texted the new one to everyone who needed to know, then logged back into the app where we'd met and sent him the messages you saw. Then, I blocked him. I wanted him to get the message: there was no way I was going to be with a cheater."

"You didn't believe his story that Vesper was his sister?"

Chantelle snorted. "How dumb did he think I was? If my brother put his hands on me where Tony's were on Vesper, I'd be calling the police. Besides, he'd literally never mentioned that he had a sister. We had been dating for four months. That's the sort of thing that comes up."

"So you'd had it."

"Yeah. I'm not going to sit around and pine after a dude who's not only been lying to me but is also going out there and getting some on the side? That's crap. I deserve better than that."

"Did you suspect anything before then?"

Chantelle shrugged. "I guess I wasn't super surprised. Tony hadn't introduced me to any of his friends or anything. I knew he lived in Paia, and he said everyone he knew was up there and that he wanted to enjoy me all to himself. Like a moron, I believed him. But in hindsight, I should have recognized that as a red flag. When I saw him with Vesper, I knew those flags were there for a reason. So I dumped him immediately."

"How did you find out who she was?"

"It's a small island. I noticed she had a prosthetic leg, and I asked around a bit. One of the fishermen who works on the docks told me her name. Said she lived in Kihei, used to be a pro surfer. That was more than enough to go on. I asked a co-worker who lived in Kihei if she knew her. She did and gave me a phone number."

"Did you call her?" I asked, raising my eyebrows.

"Nah. I didn't know if she'd be open to what I had to tell her. So I sent a text instead. Let her know what was going on, that Tony was doing both of us dirty. I figured I owed her that much, at least. Told her I'd be willing to send proof if she needed it. I know it couldn't have been easy for her to hear. If someone else had known about Tony, I would have wanted to know."

"And did Vesper reply?"

"She called me. I told her everything, and she told me the same. Said they'd been dating for almost five months, that she'd known him since he was a teenager. Said he had a habit of finding someone else and keeping multiple girlfriends at once and that she had been dumb enough to believe she could change him. I felt bad for her. She'd known him for so long, and she seemed really heartbroken about it.

"But by the end of the conversation, she was mad. She told me she was going to break up with him and thanked me for the information. A couple days later, she sent me a video of her setting fire to a photo of the two of them, and I took that to mean that she'd done it and they were broken up, but I never heard from her again. I liked her, though. Vesper was spunky. That's why I'm helping you. I don't think she should go to jail."

"What if she did it?"

Chantelle shrugged. "You're her friend. Hopefully, you'll just let it slide."

"So you don't want Tony's killer to see justice?"

"Not particularly. Given the kind of guy he was, I'm sure whoever killed him had good reason. Do you know who his current girlfriends are?"

"Girlfriend, singular. Tony seems to have finally settled down, by all accounts."

"Sure he has. That leopard that eats people's faces is *totally* not going to eat your face. It's changed."

"You don't believe he could be monogamous?"

"If it had been a one-time thing, I could *maybe* believe it. But I spoke to Vesper. I know he made a habit of playing around. Men like that, people like that, people who are chronic cheaters, there's a reason for it. They can't help themselves. They don't stop. Tony isn't going to have stopped, no matter what he told people."

"His new girlfriend gave him a kidney."

That stopped Chantelle in her tracks. "Are you serious?"

"Yeah."

"That fucker. I can't believe he would have broken her heart after that. But mark my words: if he had lived longer, he would have cheated on her, too. I can't believe he actually got that kidney. I knew he needed it. He was on the transplant list. He told he didn't have any family who could offer one. That was how I knew that whole claim about Vesper being his sister was bull. I'm not a moron. We talked about his family before specifically because of his kidneys failing and the fact that he needed a transplant. He never once mentioned a sister. Don't tell me he actually found somebody else. That's nuts."

"He did."

"Well, at least if he was killed before he thought it was okay to cheat on her, she'll never know that he eventually would have. That's good for her, at least. I mean, she must have really loved him, and I'm sure she's grieving his loss, but she won't have to deal with the loss *and* betrayal that would come from finding out he was unfaithful to her in the future."

"Do you know of anyone else who might have wanted Tony dead? Did he talk about any problems at work at all? People he wasn't getting along with? His business partner, Daniel?"

Chantelle shook her head. "Never. Tony wasn't the kind to really talk to me about his life. He wanted to know about mine, but he played his cards close to the chest. In hindsight, yes, I realize that was probably a sign things weren't on the up and up. But I didn't really think about it at the time. I just thought he was interested in me."

"So you don't know anyone who could have wanted him dead?"

"Sorry."

"Okay, thanks. Just so I can eliminate you as a suspect, can I confirm your alibi information for this morning?"

"Sure. I was at work. I'm the main administrative assistant for a boating tour company here in town. Maui Dreams Tours. Feel free to head down to the office and ask for Sandra. She was working with me all morning. You can ask her to send you some of the security footage for whatever time you're after. As long as it was after six and before two, she'll be able to cover that."

"Great. Thanks. I think that's all I've got for you. I'm going to leave you my card. If you happen to think of anything that could help me solve this, let me know, will you?"

"Sure, but as I said, I don't think I will. I haven't spoken to Tony in over a year at this point. I can tell you in general that he's a bigger piece of trash than that giant patch floating in the middle of the ocean, but I can't specifically tell you who might have wanted him dead. I imagine it's a pretty long list, though."

I said goodbye to Chantelle and headed back to Queenie, following the directions that took me to the Maui Dreams Tours office. Five minutes later, a very enthusiastic and happy-to-help Sandra had given me everything I needed to prove there was no way Chantelle had committed the murder. She had, as she'd said, been there the whole morning.

Chapter 10

I drove back home, stopping at Leoda's on the way back for a few individual pies to take home. When I entered, I found Zoe hanging out with Henry on the couch.

I immediately closed my eyes and made a big show of reaching out in front of me. "If either one of you is naked, you have until I get to the kitchen counter to get your clothes back on," I announced.

"Relax, Charlie," Zoe said. "We're not naked. We're sitting on the couch together like a normal couple, doing the crossword."

"That's not what normal couples do," I pointed out, placing the pies on the counter. I had met Henry during my last case. He ran a start-up here in Kihei that designed eco-friendly alternatives to current marine technology that were designed to help clean up the oceans. I had invited him to our

Christmas party, and he and Zoe had hit it off immediately. "If you were a normal couple, you'd be on this couch, doing it."

"If that's what you and Jake do every time you're here, he's doing something wrong, because my noise-cancelling headphones aren't *that* good," Zoe replied.

"Hey," I said, my face reddening. "We do not. Not while you're here."

Zoe laughed. "Made you blush. Turns out you *can* be embarrassed."

"It's just the heat. But all right, I'll leave the two of you here to slot the… letters… into the right boxes where they belong, then."

"Has anyone ever told you that you should write scripts for porn movies? Because that sounds like it came out of a low-budget movie from the nineties," Zoe replied.

"Thank you. But seriously, I didn't think you'd be here, so I'll take Coco for a walk."

"We can go, too, if you want," Henry offered.

I waved a hand. "Don't worry about it. I have a million things to do for this case anyway."

"Zoe was telling me about it. Another murder?" Henry shook his head sadly. "It's awful."

"Have you gotten anywhere?" Zoe asked.

"So far, it looks like the people who had the most reason to want Tony dead were his exes. The dude was a serial cheater who used his dick like a divining rod, following it along wherever it went. The problem is, he seems to have actually been monogamous with the woman he was seeing recently, especially since she gave him a kidney."

"Oh, wow."

"I'm kind of hoping someone at his job killed him, because right now, I don't have any good suspects. Except Vesper, honestly. And I don't think she killed him. But it's still early in the investigation, and it could take me in a hundred different directions. We'll see.

"I don't like the fact that everybody in his life who didn't date him seemed to think he was this amazing guy, but all the women he's ever seen hated his guts. But that's how it goes sometimes, isn't it? He was obviously a massive misogynist."

"Zoe was telling me about him. He's the guy who runs that camp for local kids, isn't he?" Henry said.

"Yeah."

"I know him. Met him a few times through my work. We spoke about the charity since I love the idea. He seemed like a good guy."

"Yeah, but only the men are the ones saying that. Even the women who knew him and didn't date him, like Leslie, don't have a lot of great things to say about him."

Henry shook his head. "Very disappointing."

"Chantelle only helped me when she found out

Vesper could go to jail if she didn't. She didn't even try to hide the fact that she wanted whoever killed him to get away with it."

"No matter what he did, we can't have a killer on the streets," Zoe said.

"Chantelle wasn't really bothered by that part," I said wryly. "But it goes to show that nothing is black and white. No one is denying that Tony's charity that got kids out surfing and on the water for free was fantastic. But his personal life was messier than a teenage boy's bedroom. Anyway, I'm sure the two of you don't want to hear about murder on your date. I'll see you later."

"Bye, Charlie. Nice to see you again," Henry said.

"You too. There's pie in the fridge that you're welcome to, as long as you leave some for me."

"Wouldn't dream of doing otherwise," Zoe said with a grin.

I grabbed Coco's leash from its hook near the door, and even though my little dog had been fast asleep on the floor, relaxing in a beam of sunshine, completely dead to the world, her sixth sense kicked in. She immediately jumped to her feet as awkwardly as her small feet and long body would let her and sprinted to the door.

The two of us headed downstairs, and Coco strained against her leash as she headed toward the beach.

"I know, I know. We're getting there. I promise," I said, breaking into a half-jog to let Coco get there faster. That was the closest I was ever going to get to running if I didn't have to.

We reached the beach, where Coco immediately buried her nose in the sand. This was her favorite thing in the world to do. She ran along the expansive stretch, and every few feet, she'd stick her face in the sand, having obviously sniffed out something incredibly interesting underneath the surface.

It was a gorgeous afternoon on Maui. Along the shore, couples, families, and individuals were hanging out under large umbrellas that offered cool shade. Children squealed as they tried body-boarding on the small waves near the shore. The rhythmic sound of the water lapping against the sand made for more soothing background noise than any YouTube video could possibly hope for. At the far end of the beach, a single honu was sunning itself; I made a mental note to make sure Coco avoided heading that way. As much as she enjoyed making new friends, getting too close to the green sea turtles was harmful to them—and very illegal.

An off-leash Jack Russel Terrier ran up to say hello. A few seconds later, he darted back off the way he had come. He found a stick about thirty feet away from us and happily carried it back to his human.

Yes, this was the perfect time to be in Hawaii.

It was the middle of winter, and in Seattle, it would be overcast at best, raining at worst. It was the time of year when I'd be willing the sun to make an appearance, even though I knew that time was still a few months away. No wonder I had hated the Pacific Northwest winters so much. This was home.

A couple of minutes later, my phone binged.

It was Rosie. *Ladies, it appears I may have a mystery of my own to solve. There's a thief in my building. But there's something strange about them.*

Strange? I replied.

The choice of what they're stealing. They've taken jewelry from two neighbors, but they've also stolen a salmon someone had out on the counter.

Crime of opportunity? That was Dot. *With inflation the way it is these days, frankly, I'd probably go for the salmon before the diamonds. Do you know how much one of those things costs at the supermarket?*

I think I found your thief, Rosie, I said, adding a tongue-sticking-out emoji to the end of the message.

Aren't you funny? It's fine. I can set up some video cameras at your complex.

Absolutely not. There's no way in the world I'm going to let anybody who lives here know that I'm anything other than a kindly old woman who has regular old-woman friends. I cannot be seen having technology or any interest in it. The other week, I pretended to ask one of my neighbors for help. I told her I'd forgotten how to unlock my phone.

Okay, so we have to do this some other way. How often is the thief striking? I typed.

I'm not one hundred percent sure. I didn't realize it was a regular occurence until today. I don't know if the rest of the building does, either. I've only just found out about it through my other neighbor and pieced it together. I suggested a thief, but she doesn't think it could be anyone in the building. They're all very naïve here. They think just because we live together, there's no way any of us could be criminals.

Is that a shot at me because I'm investigating a murder to try and clear my neighbor's name?

It is not, although the automatic assumption that Vesper is innocent just because you enjoy her company is very civilian of you.

Ouch. Like a stab to the heart.

That said, I do think your instincts about Vesper are correct. She seems to me to be a rather impulsive person without much self-control, which means she couldn't have killed Tony.

Something clicked in my brain just then. *Right. Because he was stabbed with a chef's knife. And why would anybody just have one of those hanging around at a surfing competition? They wouldn't. It had to have been brought earlier, which means the killer planned to kill him.*

Yes. And I don't think Vesper is the type of person to do that.

No. Also, when we do find a suspect, it means we've got one way of checking whether or not they're the killer. We just have to look at their knife block.

If you kill someone with your own chef's knife and you're not smart enough to get rid of the rest of the knives immediately afterwards, you deserve to go to prison for life based on stupidity alone, Dot replied.

This is why you're not a judge, I typed.

Oh, there are so many reasons why that's not the case. But I'm right. If you're going to premeditate a murder and you can't be bothered getting rid of the clear evidence that points to you, you're obviously too dumb to be a productive member of society.

And a murderer.

That too.

I feel like you think the murder is secondary.

They're both bad.

Okay, well, let's hope we got a killer missing a few brain cells, then. On the bright side, it's also turning out to be pretty easy to get alibis. The killer had to be at the competition and had to be out on the water, on a surfboard.

They likely would have had to be somewhat skilled as well, Rosie typed.

I agree. If I tried to stab someone on a surfboard, not only would I fail miserably at it, but I'd probably be the one who came out wounded.

I'm glad you're the one who said it and not me, Rosie replied.

The downside is, I was probably the only person on the water that morning who had no idea what I was doing. I'll ask Zoe if she can tell me who else was out there after she's finished filling up her box with Henry's letters.

I'm not sure I want to know what that means, Dot said.

Supposedly they're doing the crossword puzzle together.

Oh, thank goodness, Rosie replied.

I'll come over to Dot's after dinner. Rosie, write down everything you can think of regarding the thief in your building. Even if we can't use cameras, that's far from the only tool we have available when it comes to catching a thief.

I turned back to Coco, who was running along the edge of the water, diligently avoiding the waves. I couldn't blame her. She was truly my dog; she liked the beach but never wanted to go into the ocean.

After about ninety minutes of walking on the beach, Coco and I headed back home, while I wondered what Dot might have managed to dig up about Tony and his stream of girlfriends.

Chapter 11

After dinner, I headed to Dot's place once more. Rosie answered the door and let me in.

"Any luck finding more of his accounts?"

"We found his Tinder, but the account has been inactive for about a year and a half," Dot replied. "The last woman he matched with there was a tourist, and I checked. She's been on the mainland since she left. There's no way she's the killer."

I sighed. "It just doesn't make any sense. Someone like Tony, the most obvious person to kill him is the jilted girlfriend who doesn't realize she's being taken advantage of. But she doesn't seem to exist. There's only Lily, and they seem to have been in a happy, committed relationship. I'll see if I can track her down and talk to her tomorrow. I wanted to give her a bit of time to process what's happened first."

"Right. I agree. But it's also possible we're headed in the wrong direction entirely," Dot said.

"Oh?"

"I looked into Sharky Boards, the company Tony owned with Daniel."

"And?"

"Thanks to an accountant who has the worst website security known to man, I have their financial records. They weren't making nearly as much money as people thought they were. The company isn't profitable. They were keeping the lights on, but Daniel and Tony were in trouble. Neither one of them had taken a salary for six months."

"Was it profitable before?" I asked.

"Sure was. But they added too many staff members too quickly. Payroll was eating up their profits. Things were going well up until around a year and a half ago. Things got tighter for them then and only worse since."

"Where are they adding the extra staff?" Rosie asked.

"It looks like they've brought on a few more people in sales," Dot said. "And those new staff members have been bringing in some extra income, but not enough to cover what they cost. It also looks like they can't keep up with production."

"Weird. I wonder why they haven't hired more people to help make boards too," I mused.

"I don't know," Dot said.

"Daniel didn't mention any of this when I spoke to him today," I said dryly. "I wonder if it's because he realizes that a business dispute is a fantastic motive to murder your business partner. He invited me to come and speak with the employees on Monday. I'll be doing that for sure."

"And hopefully tonight, we'll find something in his home that might lead us to the killer too. You're sleeping with the detective in charge. Can you get us access to Tony's phone or anything like that?"

I laughed. "I wish. I know better than to even ask. We'll have to see what the police left at the home and use that. It's all we're going to have access to. Unless we want to break into the police evidence locker, but I think that's outside of even my comfort zone."

"Not a good idea," Rosie agreed.

"But we still have to wait a couple hours before the coast is clear. Rosie, what's going on with the thief at your place? What do you know?"

"Well, the first I heard of it was about two weeks ago. And it was from Sandra Hofstetter, who has always been a little bit on the flaky side. She said someone broke into her apartment and stole a necklace she had sitting on her bedside cabinet. Of course, I asked if she called the police, and she said yes. They came, and they had a look, but they found no signs of forced entry."

"Is it possible that Sandra left her door open?" I asked.

"Very. In fact, my initial assumption was that there wasn't a thief at all. I thought Sandra had likely simply misplaced the necklace and blamed a nonexistent thief when she couldn't find it, but in a few weeks or months, she would open a random drawer in her apartment and find it there."

"She's done that before?" I asked.

"Never to the point of accusing a thief and calling the police, but Sandra is always losing things. I know for a fact that she has her car dealership on speed dial for when she loses the keys to her Nissan. Therefore, my belief was that she had simply misplaced the necklace. However, about a week ago, another resident, John Irving, complained about a missing diamond bracelet. I found out he had left it on his dining table."

"Now things are getting more interesting," I mused.

"John swears that he locked his front door, and I'm more inclined to believe him than I am Sandra. John did admit that he left the window that leads into his dining room open, but he lives on the third floor of the building."

"So we're looking for someone who works for the circus," I said.

"Or maybe a professional snowboarder," Dot offered.

"Exactly."

"And then it's been happening a few more times. The thief never takes anything big. Just little items that are left lying around. I think it's someone in the building who is trying doors and entering apartments that are left unlocked. Or possibly windows."

"That's a common thing?" I asked. "Surely, everyone locks their doors when they leave."

"That's what I would have thought. But there are quite a few older people who live in the building who may believe they've locked their doors and simply forgotten to do it. I know I haven't; I've had a routine going nearly my entire life to ensure no one enters my apartment."

"Let me guess: your place is booby trapped so that anyone who manages to accidentally break in gets dropped into a pit of venomous snakes you keep under the floor or blown away by an elaborately rigged shotgun setup."

Rosie laughed. "Don't be ridiculous. I would never be that obvious. I use an elaborate system of magnets to trigger an alert that notifies my phone every time my front door is opened. It's a silent notification, so the criminal would be unaware that I know of their presence. Then, from my phone, I can choose to have the door locked with another set of magnets in the frame, strong enough to make it impossible to reopen. So if someone tries to break into my place, I can have them barricaded inside until the police arrive. The same system also works on the balcony door and the windows."

"Remind me never to break into your apartment."

"I would not recommend you do so."

"My home defense is simple," Dot said. "There are twenty-seven guns hidden in this apartment, and I'm the only one who knows where they are. Not to mention the security cameras. Anyone is welcome to try and steal my shit, but if they do, there are consequences."

"You're both insane. My home defense system is a dog who will immediately become best friends with any burglar who offers her a slice of pepperoni from the fridge."

"And yet you say we're the crazy ones," Dot replied.

"Although Zoe and I do both ensure the front door is locked before we go outside. So anyway, you're now pretty sure that someone actually is trying all the doors in your building, going into the open ones, and stealing whatever they can?"

Rosie nodded. "Yes. It's now happened to at least five people, so we're quite certain. The building management has put up numerous signs telling residents to ensure their doors are locked when they leave their homes over the past few weeks, but the thefts have continued."

"And the police are obviously involved at this point, I assume," I said.

"They are, but of course, they're not taking it particularly seriously. Every time another theft is reported, they come, and they take a statement, and they proceed to do nothing about it."

"Sounds about right."

"At the same time, I'm not sure what else they *can* do, short of having a presence in the halls at all times. And of course, they're never going to do that. And I'm not sure I expect them to, anyway."

"So we need to find a way to narrow down the thief. What is the security like in the building?"

"Access from the outside of the building is via a key fob. Every apartment also has a phone to let in visitors. But this isn't New York. You can't simply hit all of the buttons and hope that someone will let you in without good reason."

"Right. Plus the person who's doing this seems to be hitting only your apartment building. Is that right?"

"As far as I know."

"I should be able to find out from Jake whether there are other buildings being hit in the area, or if it's just yours," I said. "That much, he might actually tell me, especially if it helps me solve a case that he's not involved in. But let's assume you're right, and it's only your building. That would imply that whoever is doing this lives in the building."

"That is what I suspect, yes."

"Okay. Any standouts when it comes to suspects?"

"I've thought about it, but no. While the building is home to people with a variety of incomes and net worth, and there are more than a few who could likely use the money, there is nobody I can think of who stands out to me as being a potential thief. Of course, I've been keeping my eyes open, but I haven't noticed anything suspicious."

I frowned. "And if anyone would notice something, it's you."

"Yes, I believe I would. It's really quite the conundrum."

"Are all of the thefts happening during the day?"

"Mostly. A couple have been at night, with the residents asleep in the bedroom next door. Whoever it is, they are quite brazen."

"And yet this seems to be a crime of opportunity if they're only going in and taking something quick."

"Exactly."

"Has anyone new moved into your complex recently?"

"No. That's the other thing I can't figure out: why now? Why have they begun thieving as of two weeks ago? What changed? Someone must have had something in their living situation shift for them to decide they're going to steal from their neighbors," Rosie said.

"I agree. So not only do we have to look into this, but we also have to do it in such a way that no one realizes who we really are or in a way that's noticed."

"Exactly," Rosie said. "Ideally, I wouldn't be connected to this at all."

"We can make that work," Dot said. "You go about your life like everything is normal, and we can try and solve this case without involving you at all. It's not like we ever go to your place, so no one there knows that we're friends."

"Finally, Rosie's insistence on keeping her entire life more private than Howard Hughes pays off," I teased. "I'm not even sure I know where you live."

"And if it weren't for the fact that there is a criminal in our building, I'd like to keep it that way. Besides, I'd rather we find them than the police. If there's some sort of extenuating circumstances that's leading to this person thinking they have no option but to resort to theft, I would rather deal with those underlying causes directly than simply have them locked away," Rosie said.

"Okay. We'll come up with a plan. It might end up being boring—just a long stakeout—but we'll find the person doing this. Are they stealing every day?"

"No. Every few days, at least. It isn't regular; there's no pattern. I have looked."

"If this involves sitting in a car all night with nothing to do, I'm out," Dot said. "I need my beauty sleep."

"We'll see. I might have to find a way into the building. Let me think about it," I said. "Right now, though, we're going to Tony's place. It should be late enough that the cops will be gone."

"Sure will," Dot agreed. "Let's do it. See what we can find that they might have missed."

The three of us headed out and piled into Queenie, and I began the drive up to Paia.

Chapter 12

Tony had lived in a small bungalow, almost more of a shack, on the outskirts of Paia. It was located on a gravel road just off the highway, and I was glad to see there were no streetlights that might have given away our presence. He had a few neighbors nearby, but it was after midnight by the time we got there, and all of the lights were out.

A few cars were parked on the street—an older Civic, a Subaru Outback, and a small Ford Ranger. I parked behind a late-model Dodge Charger, which I took a moment to admire. I kept an eye out for Jake's Tesla, just in case, but there was no sign of it. Good. The three of us got out of the car, wordlessly and noiselessly. I pointed to the home that Google Maps told me belonged to Tony.

This part of Hawaii was well developed, with

houses on every block, but there was plenty of greenery and trees behind which we crouched to stay out of view of any neighbors who might happen to peek out of their windows right about now. If being a private investigator had taught me one thing, it was subtlety.

I wasn't exactly a ninja, but I also wasn't as careless as a hedgehog in a condom factory anymore, either. The three of us quickly reached the front door, and Dot and I stood guard while Rosie handed out latex gloves then made quick work of the lock. There was no seal on the door; obviously, the cops didn't intend to return. They must not have found much here.

Well, hopefully, we would have better luck.

The lock clicked, and the three of us entered the home. Our eyes were already somewhat adjusted to the low light, so I took a second or two to focus. We were standing in an entrance with a living room to the left and a hallway that appeared to lead to a kitchen at the back. To the right was another hallway that I presumed went to the bedrooms.

Rosie immediately paused when we closed the door behind us. "Someone has been here recently," she said, her voice so low it was almost noiseless.

"Yeah, the cops," I replied. "We don't know when they left."

"Do you still want to do this?" Dot asked Rosie.

"I'm fine. But I think we should be extremely careful. Charlie, take the living room. Dot, you're on kitchen and dining. I'll take the bedroom."

I gave a curt nod and immediately headed to the living room on the left. My senses were all on high alert. Rosie was good at this sort of thing, so if she thought someone had been here recently, she was probably right.

She must have been thinking about the police. Even though it was late at night, this was a murder. I knew Jake wouldn't stop working tonight. I knew he was probably at the station now, hunched over his desk, trying to find Tony's killer while Liam shot stupid questions across the table.

Like what time Krispy Kreme closed.

Turning on the lights would have been *way* too suspicious, and I didn't want any neighbors calling the cops. I went to the main windows that looked out onto the street and pulled the drapes closed then turned on my phone's camera. I scanned the room and took it all in. Tony's living room was rather minimalist. There was a wall-mounted TV on the left-hand side, a desk near the window, and a small bar against the wall that backed against the kitchen. Across from the TV was a couch with a man sitting on it.

Wait, what?

I shined the light back at the couch, where Jake

was sitting, staring at me with a "Are you fucking kidding me right now?" expression on his face.

"Well, hello, fancy seeing you here," I said, flashing him the biggest smile I could. I was in *so* much trouble.

"Charlie."

"Jake. Taking a break from your murder investigation?"

"I wish I was. No, I came here half an hour ago, wondering if maybe there was something I missed. Imagine my surprise when I heard a sound at the door. Could it be a clue? The killer, coming to find evidence of their crime and destroy it? But no, it's my girlfriend, breaking and entering into someone's home."

"Does it count as breaking and entering when they're dead? I mean, it's not like Tony is using it."

"Yes. *And* it's a crime scene."

"There's no seal on the door."

"Because I removed it. There *was* a seal."

"You can't expect me to know that."

"Okay. So you *only* broke into a guy's home when it wasn't a crime scene."

"Technically not his home anymore."

"I can't believe this."

"I'm a private investigator. I have to do what's right for my client."

"And let me guess: Rosie and Dot are here with you."

"Absolutely not. This one was all me."

"I heard you talking to someone when you entered."

"I talk to myself sometimes. I find it relaxes me and helps me think when I'm looking for evidence as to who committed a crime. Besides, you came in here."

"I'm a police officer who's officially investigating this murder. I'm allowed to do it. I can't believe you're making me explain that."

"I should be allowed to do it too. I might not be a cop, but I'm also officially investigating this murder. I'm doing it on behalf of Vesper and not the people on Maui, but I feel like it's a little bit of a po-tay-to, po-tah-to situation."

"You should try and use that as your defense in front of the judge. See how well that goes for you."

"Oh please. You're not going to arrest me."

Jake stared me down for a minute, and I matched his gaze. There was no way he was going to arrest me. Right?

"Fine," he finally admitted, rolling his eyes. "I'm not going to arrest you."

"Because I'm adorable?"

Jake shot me *a look*. "Because I don't think it would serve the course of justice. And because I don't think our relationship would survive it, and as much as I don't understand why at this moment, I want to keep dating you."

"It's because I've got spunk."

"That you do. You broke into a dead guy's house less than twenty-four hours after his murder."

"Why are you working this late at night, anyway? Why are you here?"

"Because someone killed him, and the first forty-eight hours are the most important. I keep wondering if we missed something. I thought I would come by here and check. I didn't expect to find you. Are you *sure* your old friends aren't here somewhere too? Because this sounds like the sort of thing you would have done with them. Zoe would have tried to talk you out of it, though."

"That's true, Zoe would have. But it's past Dot and Rosie's bedtime. This one's just me. I figured I could take my time looking around, see what the cops missed, and use that to find the killer."

"You're not going to find anything here. We gave it a very thorough look earlier. And I just spent an hour going through it all."

"Where's your car, anyway? I looked for your Tesla, just in case."

Jake grinned. "I traded it in yesterday. I was going to tell you at dinner tonight and ask you if you wanted to go for a ride in it."

I swore under my breath. "I wouldn't have come in here if I'd known you were here."

"I know that. Just another advantage of the new car."

"Why did you trade it in?"

"It was giving me a few issues, so I felt it was time. I like the Charger. It's got some oomph to it."

"It is a sweet ride. I like it. You need to give me a heads-up on these things, though."

"Why? So you don't get caught by your boyfriend breaking the law?"

"Exactly."

"You're impossible."

"So, what did you find here today?"

Jake shook his head. "Are you serious? I'm not telling you. That's confidential police information."

"Come on. We're both after the same thing here. A killer. I spoke to another one of Tony's exes today. He found her on a dating site about a year ago. She's the one who told Vesper about him after she found out that they weren't as exclusive as she thought they were."

Jake raised an eyebrow. "That was good of her to do."

"I agree. She definitely held a grudge, but I also confirmed her alibi. There's no way she could have done it."

"You're looking into his exes, then?"

I nodded. "That seems to be the most obvious way to go. The guy had a list of exes longer than the line at the post office two weeks before Christmas."

"None of them are recent, though," Jake pointed out.

"That's true, and that's the issue we're running into," I admitted. "Daniel, his business partner, invited me to come over to the factory on Monday to meet with his employees. Daniel is on the suspect list too. We know that company isn't making nearly as much money as he says it is."

"Oh? How do you know that?"

"Hey, I told you something. Now you have to tell *me* something. That's how this works."

"That is not at all how this works. I'm the cop. You have to tell me what you know, and I don't have to tell you anything."

"In that case, I invoke the Twenty-First Amendment."

"The Twenty-First?"

"That's the one that says, 'I don't have to tell you anything.' Cops always pretend that they're all-powerful, when really, I was being nice and trying to work with you."

"The Twenty-First Amendment marks the end of Prohibition."

"Are you serious? Who actually *knows* that stuff? I just made up an amendment."

A small smile curled in the corner of Jake's mouth. "Just us all-powerful cops. You know, the people who are supposed to uphold the law. Like amendments to the Constitution."

"Oh please, if I asked Liam what the Twenty-First Amendment was, he'd probably tell me what combo number twenty-one at Burger King is."

"Well, I think it's important stuff for me to know, at least. Now, we're getting off topic. How do you know the company is doing badly?"

"I'm not going to tell you if you aren't going to share what you've found out," I said, crossing my arms.

"I can't tell you. I would get in so much trouble."

"Who would ever know? I'm not going to tattle."

"Still. The risks are too high. Sorry, Charlie. Now come on, let's get out of here. It's been a very long day, and I have to go back to the station and keep going."

"Fine. But you have to tell me what you found here, or else I'm going to keep coming back, and you're not going to be able to keep tabs on me forever. And you don't want to explain to your boss why you need an officer stationed in front of this property twenty-four seven."

Jake sighed. "You're impossible, you know that?"

"I'm trying to find a killer."

"Me too."

"Then let's work together."

Jake pressed two fingers to the bridge of his nose. "I can't believe I'm actually considering this.

135

But fine. If I tell you this, though, you need to *promise* that you are not going to break into this home again. And if I find you here, girlfriend or not, I am arresting you."

"Deal."

"Okay. Fine. Someone was blackmailing Tony."

I raised my eyebrows. "What over?"

"We don't know. The messages didn't say. But he kept them all in a box on his desk. They're all typed messages from someone, telling him that if he doesn't pay, they'll reveal his secret."

"And there's no telling what that secret is?"

Jake shook his head. "I get the feeling the person sent him some proof, and Tony destroyed that. All the messages he kept are cryptic about what the secret actually is."

"Are there instructions on how he was supposed to leave the money?"

Jake nodded. "Yup. He was supposed to go up to the parking lot for the Acid War Trail, up by Nakalele Blowhole. He was told to leave the package under a certain rock at a specific time and then drive off. The time given was early—seven in the morning."

"That's smart," I said, nodding. "That part of the island is so isolated then, if the blackmailer was watching, they would easily be able to see him and just him and notice if he brought anyone else along."

"Exactly. And if he wanted to do something like drop a spy camera, there's very limited cell service up there, so it would have been much harder to do. Whoever was blackmailing him was smart."

"How much did they take him for?"

"Ten grand so far. At least, from the notes we have. It could be more."

"Do you have any clues as to who they're from?"

Jake shook his head. "I ordered them sent off for forensics testing, but I don't know what they're going to find out beyond maybe the model of printer that was used. They're literally just typed messages in a basic font, maybe Arial. Size twelve."

"Damn. I guess it was too much to hope for that they'd sign their name with a flourish at the bottom."

"Right. So I don't know how we're going to get any further with that, but it's certainly something."

I nodded. "Okay. Do you think the killer is the blackmailer?"

"I don't know," Jake said slowly.

"The problem with blackmailing someone and then murdering them is that if Tony was paying, their fun new income source dries up."

"That's what I'm thinking as well. There were no messages indicating that Tony was doing anything other than paying the person blackmailing him. Something would have had to change, I think, for the blackmailer to kill him."

"Maybe Tony found out who it was," I suggested. "If it was somebody close to him, especially someone big in the surfing community, maybe they decided that killing Tony was the safest way to go. Maybe they thought he would reveal their identity and ruin their reputation in the community. Or go to the cops."

"That's possible," Jake said. "I wish we knew what the blackmail was over too."

"Either way, Tony's life seems to get messier and messier the more we dig into it. I initially thought the exes might be the way to go, but I don't know anymore."

"I think it was someone he was romantically linked to. I hate to have to tell you this, but Vesper is still one of the main suspects."

"She shouldn't be. She didn't kill him."

"Every murderer has neighbors. Just because we happen to know Vesper doesn't mean she isn't a killer."

"And just because she had a reason to kill him doesn't mean she did it."

"I'm not saying she did. I'm not arresting her yet. But I'm focusing on Tony's personal life. I think this blackmail probably has something to do with that too."

"Do you think he was being monogamous with Lily?" I asked.

Jake frowned. "I don't know. I haven't heard any indication otherwise. You?"

I shook my head. "No. And honestly, I'm inclined to believe it. I think he probably would have *eventually* cheated on Lily but was a decent enough person to at least give monogamy a shot after she gave him a kidney. Like, come on. You'd have to be a *real* terrible human being to cheat on someone almost immediately after they did that for you."

"I agree. But Tony has left so many exes in his wake. We don't know what might have happened that could have triggered some old feelings. Maybe one of them got angry that he finally seemed to have settled down. And that's why I still suspect Vesper."

"Fine. Well, you can go that way in your investigation. I'm going to keep an open mind, and that means not instantly blaming the woman I live next to."

"That's not keeping an open mind. That's deciding you don't want your friend to be the killer," Jake pointed out.

"Close enough."

"Literal opposites."

"Okay. Thanks for the heads-up on the blackmail."

"I hate that I tell you these things. I really am not supposed to. But you promised you're not going to come back here. And if you get caught, I'm not going to be able to bail you out."

"Yes, I promise. Understood. I'm leaving."

"Good. And goodnight, Rosie and Dot. I'm sure you're hiding somewhere."

Chapter 13

J ake and I left Tony's home. Where were Dot and Rosie, I wondered? Obviously, they'd gotten out without Jake hearing them. But I was still going to have to give them a ride back to Kihei.

"So this is the new ride, huh?" I said, motioning to the Charger I'd parked in front of. "Is it black? I can't really tell in the dark."

"Sure is."

"Badass. I bet she'd be great on the highway. Well, it's not exactly the date I had in mind, but I'm glad we got to spend some time together tonight after all," I said with a wink, grabbing the handle to open Queenie's driver's-side door.

"You're the most impossible person I've ever dealt with."

"Thank you."

"That wasn't a compliment."

"Close enough."

"Literal opposites." I slid into the driver's seat, and Jake came over, closing the door and leaning against the frame. "I know this isn't the first murder you've investigated, but be careful, okay, Charlie? I don't know who killed Tony or who was blackmailing him or even if they were the same person, but there's at least one person in his life who was willing to break the law. And one who was willing to kill."

"I know. I'm being careful."

"You literally broke into a home that had a person sitting on the living room couch that you didn't notice for a solid two minutes."

"Well, you should have made some noise."

"I mean it, Charlie."

"And you have to understand that this is my job, and I'm not always terrible at it. I'll be careful. No one has murdered me yet, and it hasn't been for a lack of trying."

"Fine. I'll call you tomorrow night, okay? I think it's going to be a few days before we can reschedule that date, though. Sorry."

"It's all good. I get it. I really do. You're a cop, and that comes with weird hours and dangerous cases, and sometimes we're not going to be able to go out when we planned on short notice. You don't have to apologize for it. I knew what I signed up for."

Jake offered me a small smile. "Thanks. I know. It's just, sometimes, when you meet someone, the *idea* of cop hours and the reality of cop hours are two different things."

"Yeah, but I'm obviously much cooler than all your exes."

"They committed far fewer crimes."

"That you know of."

"Okay, good night, Charlie. Please just go home, and don't commit any more felonies."

"I won't," I promised. I started the car, put it into drive, and pulled back out onto the Hana Highway. I got about a half mile down the road, pulled into side street, and grabbed my phone. There was already a text from Rosie; I had put the phone on silent before we'd reached Tony's place, just to be safe.

Don't worry about us. Dot had a friend in the neighborhood. We're at her place now. If you haven't come to get us by morning, we'll come bail you out from jail.

She listed the address, and I punched it into my phone. Ten minutes later, the three of us were driving back toward Kihei.

"I *knew* there was someone in there," Rosie said, shaking her head. "You all thought I was crazy."

"Okay, I will admit, we learned a lesson," I replied. "Or at least, I did. Rosie is still way, way better at this sort of thing than me. How did you know?"

"I could sense them. And there was a scent on the air. You know, like lingering body spray?"

"Seriously, you could smell that?" Dot asked.

"It's important to train your body to be able to. Knowing when you're in another person's presence can be the difference between life and death. It's good to see you weren't arrested, at least."

"Yeah, and I'm glad the two of you got out okay. I figured if one of us got caught, it might as well be me. I know he doesn't believe that I was alone, but he didn't call me out on it too badly, so you never know. I assume the two of you didn't have time to find anything good?"

"As soon as I heard you talking, I bailed out the back," Dot said. "But Rosie didn't."

Rosie, in the passenger seat next to me, shrugged. "I figured we were already there. And as soon as you told him you were by yourself, he would have stopped listening out. Or assumed we'd left. So I did search the bedroom before climbing out the window and meeting back up with Dot."

"Did you find anything?"

"A hidden camera, set up in the frame of the window. Very small; I can see why the police missed it. I grabbed it, and it looks like the connection is wireless. I'm hoping Dot can track down the details of the person who put it there."

"I'll have a look when we get home," Dot said.

"I found out from Jake that someone was blackmailing Tony. He doesn't know about what, but if someone had a hidden camera pointed to his bedroom, that might explain it," I said.

"If that were the case, wouldn't Tony have found the camera and torn it out if the person sent him photos from there?" Dot asked.

"It was right in the window frame," Rosie said. "The angle of the camera means any photo or video taken by the camera could have looked like it was taken from a phone camera outside pointing in. Tony might have simply thought that was it and not thought to look closer. But the camera was small. Tiny. I don't think anyone other than me would have spotted it."

"Okay. Let's hope we can find out who the camera belongs to, then. I don't know if the blackmailer is going to turn out to be the killer, but even if they aren't, they might know something about Tony that could lead us to the person who is."

"I think they're going to be the same person," Dot said.

"You do?" I asked. "But if the person who was blackmailing Tony killed him, then they lose their stream of money."

"Sure, but what are the odds of there being two

people out there willing to commit crimes at Tony's expense? Because let's face it, murder is worse, but blackmail is still a crime. It's a risk. And there's a chance the person would get caught, reported to the police, and spend time in jail. Some people might hang around with a whole host of criminals, but Tony seemed to lead a relatively normal life. Crime-wise, anyway. I'm not talking about the philandering."

I nodded. "Okay, I see what you're saying. You think the odds of someone like Tony running into two different people willing to commit crimes against him are low."

"Yeah. Sure, he has a bunch of exes, and they aren't thrilled with him. But most people, when they break up with someone, they move on. They don't secretly install a camera in his house to spy on them and blackmail them."

"Oh yeah? What's the worst thing you've ever done to an ex?"

"Joe was the worst I ever had. I was married to the guy, for goodness' sake. If there was ever anyone I would have wanted dead, it would be him. But when I got my freedom from him, when I finally found the courage to leave, that was it. I was so happy to be on my own, to finally be able to live my life on my own terms, that he could have done whatever he wanted and I couldn't have cared less."

"Sure, but that's because you felt trapped with him. What about anyone else you dated? After Joe. Or before. People you wouldn't have married but that you felt close to."

Dot considered my words. "Okay, well, I didn't date much after Joe. He kind of ruined the idea of men for me, you know? But before him, in my twenties, there were a couple."

"And they ended badly?"

"One did. I found out he was cheating on me," Dot admitted. "After I'd moved to Alaska for him."

"And did you keep tabs on him after you broke up?"

"No. But I got my revenge the day we split. He always wanted to go hiking. A real outdoorsy type, John was. It wasn't for me. It's like walking, only harder. And don't even get me started on winter."

"You're truly a woman after my own heart," I said with a grin.

"Anyway, that morning, I made a batch of granola bars, but I laced them with laxatives. I gave them to him when we started going, and he was thrilled. Ate them all up. You can guess what happened next."

"Oh, gross," I said, scrunching up my face while Rosie laughed.

"We got about forty-five minutes in before things started going badly for him. And it was *bad*.

He ended up on the ground, crying. I told him he deserved it, and that's what happens to cheaters. Then I walked back down to the trailhead, and it was the best hike I'd ever been on."

I was howling with laughter at this point. "What happened to him? Did you ever find out?"

"I flew back to Hawaii that afternoon. I found out from the couple of friends I had that he was heartbroken. I was really proud of myself. Last I heard, he was in Idaho. Or maybe it was Iowa. Either way, he was out of my life."

"I can't believe you had the guts to try that," I said, shaking my head. "I could never."

"I just wish I'd been that brave when I saw the red flags with Joe," Dot said. "A moment of strength combined with the invincibility of youth, I suppose. But all of that to say, six months after I'd broken up with that guy, I had basically straight-up forgotten about him. Sure, things between us had gone to shit —literally—but I moved on. He could have come back to the island, and I wouldn't have given a hoot. I certainly wouldn't have been at his window, secretly installing cameras to spy on him."

"I wonder if there's more than one," I mused. "After all, Rosie only got to check the bedroom. But it's possible the person who did this hid more. Maybe there's one in the living room."

"I would need to go back and have a look, but it

would be smart to wait a few days," Rosie said. "After all, I assume Jake wouldn't be thrilled to find any of us back there."

"No. He made it very clear that if he catches me there again, he will arrest me, and I'm pretty sure that applies to you, too."

Rosie snorted. "I'd love to see him try. But that said, we know of at least one camera. We don't need to look for more, whether or not they exist."

"Yeah. There's a blackmailer out there. Dot, do you think you can get information off it?"

"I'm not sure yet. This is very small, and it's certainly using wireless technology to transmit its data. There's no physical SD card or anything like that. But how easily I'll be able to trace it to someone will depend. I'll have to have a closer look when I get home."

"Either way, I don't think tonight was a waste at all," I said.

"No, it certainly wasn't," Rosie agreed. "I find most times, when you're doing things in the middle of the night, they're not a waste."

"Spoken like a true former spy."

"Of course, Charlie probably had a different idea as to what she wanted to do with Jake in the middle of the night tonight," Dot teased.

I was glad it was night time and neither one of them could see the blush that crawled up my face.

"Oh, come on. You're not teenagers. You can't make fun of me for that anymore," I complained.

"We absolutely can, especially since it totally embarrasses you," Dot replied. "I find it funny. Anyway, Jake is good for you. Apart from the fact that he won't let you see murder evidence. If he did, you should propose to him straight away. That would make for a great husband."

"I think the fact that he is a police officer who is unwilling to allow his private investigator girlfriend to look through evidence of a crime is, in fact, a mark in Jake's favor," Rosie countered. "Although I will admit it does make our lives slightly more difficult."

"If it weren't for Jake hiding stuff from us, we wouldn't have had to go out tonight," I pointed out.

"Those are all good points," Dot said as I pulled into her building's parking lot. "Are you coming up? I don't know how long it's going to take for me to get some information out of this bad boy, but if we're lucky, I might have a name pretty quickly."

The three of us headed upstairs. As soon as we entered Dot's apartment, I went straight to the couch, while Dot went to her desk and pulled out a small box of tools.

"Do you think there's a tracking device in that thing?" I asked. "Or is it still recording? Maybe the killer heard our whole conversation in the car."

"I doubt it," Dot said. "Technology that would

work *that* well would need a larger physical footprint. If this little thing can, then we're probably looking for someone who works for the NSA. Or who's stolen their stuff."

"In that case, I'm sure we'd see Lucy, our friendly local CIA agent, sniffing around," I said with a grin.

"My initial instincts were right. There's no physical data storage on this camera, which means everything was being transmitted somewhere," Dot said. She pulled out one of those little magnifying glasses used by jewelers and began examining the device.

Rosie went to the kitchen and grabbed a glass of water. She held one up to me in question, but I shook my head.

"This uses Bluetooth," Dot announced.

"Okay, but so do my headphones. And if I get more than about thirty feet away from my phone, the connection conks out," I pointed out. "Wouldn't that be the same here? How was the person spying on Tony if they had to be within thirty feet of that camera?"

"Not all Bluetooth devices are built the same," Dot replied. "Most headphones and other basic Bluetooth devices you would use for your phone are class two. Basically, that means they have a range of about thirty feet, and they transmit at 2.5 mW. There's also class three, which has an even shorter range. But there's also class one. And after that, you're dealing with other technology, like repeaters, that can extend the range of Bluetooth even farther."

"How much range would a class-one object have?" I asked.

"Around three hundred feet, give or take. Like with anything else, Bluetooth connections can be affected by things like walls. Since this camera was located in an interior wall, I would expect that the range would have been shortened because of that. But this is a class-one device for sure. The data was collected by the camera and sent wirelessly via Bluetooth to another device nearby."

"Within three hundred feet of Tony's home," I mused. "An upset neighbor?"

"It's possible. But it might not have been, either. The data wouldn't have to be sent to a computer; a smartphone would have been fine. In fact, that's how I suspect this was done. A phone would have been hidden near the property, connected to a power source outside, and collected all of the video from the wireless camera. Then, the person who put it there likely would have just had to log onto an app from home to see what they found."

I blew air up into my bangs. "Does that mean we can track them? And by we, I, of course, mean you."

Dot pursed her lips. "Maybe. We'll see. If we

were able to find the phone, absolutely. That wouldn't be a problem at all."

"A lot of houses have a few outdoor electrical sockets. I wonder if the person plugged the phone into one of them, thinking the owners might not use them, especially not for long enough that they'd be noticed anytime soon," I mused. "Actually, I just had an even worse thought: what if the phone was plugged in at *Tony's* house? That would be so close the Bluetooth connection would definitely be strong enough. But then the cops would have found it."

Rosie nodded. "That's a risk. But we don't know for sure. Tomorrow, I will go back to Tony's neighborhood. I can ask the local residents if anyone has found a phone. Nobody ever suspects an old lady of anything nefarious."

"Good idea," I said. "Besides, Dot and I also have to look into that thief that's hitting up your place."

"I'll see if I can track anything on this end, too," Dot said. "I might still be able to find out who that camera belonged to. But it would be significantly easier if I had the phone. There isn't any identifying data on this camera. I don't know what company produced it or what app they're using for the data transfer. But of course, it's only been ten minutes. We'll see what I can dig up."

"In that case, I'm going to go home and try to

get some sleep," I said. "We'll connect in the morning."

I really hoped Dot was going to find who was spying on Tony, because either they were the killer or they might be able to lead us in the right direction.

Chapter 14

I woke up the next morning to the sound of a text message coming in. Blinking away the sleep, trying to figure out what time it was, I grabbed my phone. It was just after eight in the morning, which meant I'd probably gotten a little less than six hours of shut-eye.

The text was from Dot. Did she ever sleep?

Rosie has gone to see the neighbors. I'm still getting nowhere with this stupid camera. But worse than that, I have some news. Another Ham brother associate is getting on a plane to Hawaii. They booked it for this afternoon.

My heart sank as I read the words. *Here's hoping it's just another one going on a tropical vacation. But we'll keep an eye on him.*

Good. That's what I'm thinking too. And we have to go check out Rosie's place. I got us started on that. There's an apartment in her building up for sale, so I got in touch with a real estate agent friend of mine. She's going to organize a viewing, and we can go from there.

Sounds like a plan. Pretending you're going to buy a place is a great way to ask questions without raising suspicion.

My thoughts exactly. I'll let you know when the details are locked in.

Cool. Thanks.

I headed into the kitchen to find a note from Zoe, letting me know that she had already walked *and* fed Coco, no matter how much my dog tried to convince me otherwise. I looked down at my dog's big brown eyes as they looked up at me, desperately trying to tell me she hadn't had breakfast yet, and that she was starving and neglected.

"Sorry, chunko. Zoe already told me you've had breakfast. You can't slip one past us like that. The people can talk to each other. And you have tiny little legs. If you get fat, your stomach is just going to drag on the ground. Is that what you want?"

"That's definitely the goal," was what Coco's little eyes said as she jumped up on me, giving me her best begging face.

After a couple of minutes, Coco realized she wasn't going to get any extra breakfast. I grabbed one of the pies I'd bought at Leona's the other day and headed over to the couch. Coco immediately followed me, practically screaming "sharing is caring" at me. She sat on the couch, staring expectantly at my plate, her little tail wiggling from side to side along the fabric like a windshield wiper going in a hurricane.

"You're lucky you're cute," I said as I broke a small chunk of crust from the edge of the pie and handed it to her. Coco immediately wolfed it down as if she hadn't eaten in days.

After breakfast, I still hadn't heard from Dot, so I figured I would continue on my quest to find out who had killed Tony. I had gotten Lily's phone number from Daniel yesterday, so I began up a new message. I figured if she wasn't up for chatting, a text would be less invasive.

Hi, Lily. My name is Charlotte Gibson, and I'm investigating Tony's death separately from the police. I'm really sorry for your loss. I'm wondering if you'd be willing to talk to me about him, just so I can better understand what was going on in his life and hopefully be able to find his murderer. I understand if this is too soon for you, but it could really help me bring his killer to justice. Thanks.

I sent the message and hopped into the shower while I waited for a reply. My phone binged just as I was drying myself off.

You're looking into Tony's death? So who are you working for? I can meet with you this morning if you're trying to find who killed him.

I'm working for Vesper, his ex. She's one of my neighbors. But I'm after the truth. If she did this, she deserves to go to jail. Where do you want to meet?

I'd rather meet in public. Wailuku Coffee? In, say, an hour?

Great. I'll be there.

I had been to Wailuku Coffee a couple of times. It was pretty close to the hospital where Zoe worked, and we'd gone there for coffee and snacks when meeting up after her shifts. I said goodbye to Coco, grabbed my bag, and headed down to the drive up to Kahului.

Wailuku Coffee was right on the street. I found a parking spot about a block away and walked inside, joining the end of the short line of people waiting to be served. The place was cute and had a bit of a rustic vibe. The main counter was wood, with the menu on a chalkboard behind it. There were a few seats inside, to the right, under an exposed brick arch, and I thought maybe Lily would prefer the added privacy of being indoors. I found a small chair and table for two in the far corner and took my white chocolate mocha there, waiting for her to arrive.

I spotted Lily about five minutes later and waved to catch her eye when she looked around for me. She nodded, waited in line, and arrived with her coffee a not long afterwards.

"Charlotte?" she asked.

"Yeah. But you can call me Charlie. Everyone does."

She nodded and sat down. It was obvious Lily

had been crying. Her auburn hair hadn't seen a brush in quite a while, and her eyes were red-rimmed and puffy. She wore a simple graphic T-shirt and a pair of shorts, and she stared into the coffee, wrapping her hands around it as if the warmth of the cup could fill the hole in her heart.

I knew how she felt.

"I'm sorry about Tony," I said quietly.

"Thank you. It was a shock. I can't believe it. How could this happen? Who could have done this?"

"That's what I'm trying to find out. Thank you for meeting me."

"He was a good person. That's what I want you to know," she said, finally meeting my eyes. "He was the best. I loved him so much. Do you know that he ran a camp for local kids so they would get the opportunity to learn to surf? They didn't have to pay for a thing. He went out with them on Saturday mornings, twenty-eight weeks a year."

"I heard about that," I said with a smile.

"Everyone loved him. He made such a difference in the community. Everyone who surfed was such good friends with him. He taught me to surf, you know? When we met, I had no idea how to do it. I grew up in Oregon. My parents moved to Oahu when I was a teenager, and at that point, I was at the age where I was too cool to learn something new. But Tony, he was so patient with me."

"That's special. You should hang on to that," I said.

"Thanks. I will. It's hard, though. I'm not sure I can go back to the water without remembering yesterday." Lily shuddered. "It all feels like a bit of a blur now."

"Can you walk me through the day? You were both competing?"

"Yes. Tony did it every year, and this was going to be my first. I didn't have any expectations for myself, of course. I just wanted to go out there and have some fun. I'd never seen Tony compete, though, but I knew he'd have a good chance at winning his age category."

"So he wasn't competing in the professional group?"

"No. Not anymore. Tony retired from competitive surfing decades ago. Most of the people in his age group were former pro athletes, though. So it was still going to be tough for him to win, but I knew he could do it. He still had that desire to win inside of him, even if it wasn't a world title he was going for anymore but just a cute ceramic pineapple riding a surfboard.

"We got there early in the morning, at around six. Tony always chatted with people before he went out, and he wanted time to warm up. Sure enough, as soon as we got there, he started talking with the organizers. They were old friends of his, so I got our boards out, set everything up, and waited for a bit of light before going out. As soon as it was light enough, Tony and I entered the water together. We split up pretty quickly, though. Different waves and all that. Plus he's so much better than I am. I had to focus on what I was doing and try not to mess up. Or hit other people. The ocean got busy pretty quickly."

I nodded. "Yeah. I was there. I agree."

"Anyway, I let Tony go do his own thing while I worked on my tricks for the day. I don't know how much time passed, but eventually, I saw a commotion out by the shore. I thought maybe someone had gotten hurt, so I went in. And that… that was when I saw it. I saw the board. I would have known it anywhere. He built that board himself. And I looked over… almost immediately, someone grabbed me and made me turn away, but I'd seen him. And I knew."

Tears welled in Lily's eyes, and she swallowed hard. "Someone had killed Tony. They murdered him with a knife to the back. I couldn't breathe. It felt like someone had stabbed me too. I don't know what happened. Someone led me away from the scene and sat me down. Some EMTs came by, and they took care of me for a while. Then Daniel came over. He drove me home. He was so kind. He said that he would take care of everything and that I wouldn't have to worry. He called me last night just to see how I was doing. And he brought me food. That was nice. But this whole time, I've just been asking myself one thing: who could have done this to Tony? And I keep coming up empty."

"Can I ask about you? And your relationship?"

"If you think it will help. But Tony and I were happy. Really happy."

"I know. I'm just hoping that the more I learn about Tony and every aspect of his life, the closer I can get to finding the killer."

Lily nodded. "It's not fair, you know? He got a new lease on life six months ago. I gave him a kidney. Did you know that?"

"Daniel told me."

"Do you know what the odds were that we would be a match? Infinitesimally small. Almost zero. We met because a cousin of mine needs a transplant too. She was in a car accident that shredded her kidneys about a year ago. I wanted to see if we matched, obviously. We didn't, but luckily, her sister did. But that was where I met Tony. He was on dialysis, and even though it was obviously hell for him, he was still in good spirits. He kept making jokes, which I liked. Then I saw him when I visited Jessica a few days later, once I found out she was getting her surgery. That was when he asked me out."

"And you said yes?" I asked with a smile.

"Yeah. I figured why not, you know? I never

really had a thing for older guys, but Tony was nice. And it's not like I had to marry the guy. So I agreed, and we went on a couple of dates. We hit it off straight away, and the next thing I knew, we were serious."

"Did he ask you to get tested to donate your kidney?"

Lily shook her head. "No. I suggested it. Tony would never. In fact, he almost tried to stop me. He didn't want me to donate a kidney. He said I was too young, that he could wait it out on the transplant list for a few more years. But I insisted. After all, if there was a chance, even a tiny one, that it could work, I wanted to do that for him. And lo and behold, it did. I don't think anyone was more surprised than Tony."

"He must have been happy."

"You would think so, but he tried to stop me again. Repeated that I was young, and he didn't want me taking that risk. He said he cared about me too much. But eventually, I told him that if he really cared about me, he would let me do this for him because I cared about him too. And that I couldn't watch him waste away, knowing that I could fix his pain by giving him one of my kidneys."

"So he got the transplant."

"Yeah. The recovery was hard, but it was worth it."

"Did anyone tell you about Tony's past relationships?"

Lily nodded. "A couple of his female friends did. They told me Tony had a history of cheating on the women he was with. I met a few of his exes as well through the surfing world. Vesper, the woman you're working for, she was one of them, I think. She's the one with one leg, right?"

"That's her."

"Yeah. She seems nice. Look, I'm not an idiot. I know that people cheat, and I knew we had only been in a relationship for a few months. But I also know that sometimes, people meet the person that's really right for them. And that's what happened with us. I spoke to Tony about it. I told him if we were going to be together, we had to be exclusive. And I didn't want to be with someone who couldn't be loyal to me."

"What did he say to that?"

"He admitted everything. He said that he had been bad in the past and that he had betrayed the women he was with. He promised that would never happen with me, though, because he could tell that I was different. He felt a connection with me that he'd never had before. He said that he felt absolutely no desire to wander and that if I didn't trust him yet, that was fine. We could always wait to do the surgery if I didn't want to go ahead because of his history."

"But you didn't wait?"

"No. I believed him. And besides, I know it was a big thing to give someone a kidney, but it's not as if that tied us together for life. It's not a wedding. I knew there was a chance that after I gave him that kidney, things could change between us. I didn't give it to him as a way to keep him attached to me for life. But at the same time, I knew we were meant to be together. I saw myself spending the rest of my life with him, and I think he saw the same. He had even brought up the idea of engagement a couple of times in the last few weeks." Lily smiled sadly as she gazed into her almost-untouched coffee.

"What is it that you do for work?"

"Public service. I work for the state government."

"Do you know much about Tony's work? Anybody he might have been having problems with? Were things going well for him there?"

Lily shook her head. "Everything was fine. Tony would tell me about it. He said Sharky Boards was really taking off and that in ten years, they'd be as well-known a company in the surfing world as the other major players. That was one of the things that originally drew me to him; he was a businessman, an established one. He had big goals for his business, and he was going to hit them."

Okay, so Tony was hiding the fact that Sharky Boards was bleeding money from the people in his life as well. That wasn't a huge surprise; no one wanted to admit to their loved ones that their business wasn't doing great. But it was still good to know.

"He never mentioned problems with anybody? How about Daniel, his business partner?"

Lily bit her lip as she thought about my question and shook her head slowly. "No. I'm trying to think, but I really, genuinely can't think of anything Tony mentioned involving Daniel, or anyone from work, being a problem. I wish I could. Actually, wait."

"Yes?"

Lily started nodding slowly. "About a week ago, actually, Tony mentioned something. It was just in passing, so I didn't really think much of it at the time, you know? It wasn't even that bad. But now that you mention it, well…"

"What is it?"

"Tony said to me that he was worried about Daniel. They had a strategy meeting a couple of weeks ago where they went over all of their numbers in the business. Tony said Daniel was afraid to grow. He said a lot of people are, that it's a mindset issue. But that they disagreed with the direction the two of them should be taking. Tony wanted to be aggressive. He wanted them to take advantage while they were growing and push even further. But Daniel wanted them to pull back on some of the changes they were making. He wanted them to press the pause button on the business, essentially. Tony disagreed. But that was all it was. A disagreement between business partners. I really don't think Daniel would actually *kill* over that, do you?"

I shrugged. "In my experience, people will kill over things the rest of us would normally consider ridiculous. Do you know who else was on the water that morning?"

Lily blew air out from her cheeks. "Oh, I can try. I'm not entirely sure, though. There were a lot of people I didn't recognize at all, since I'm not big into the surfing scene outside of Tony. But Tony was there, obviously. There was also a doctor from the hospital. I recognized her."

"That's Zoe Morgan. She's my best friend and the one who was teaching me how to surf. She found Tony's body along with me."

"Okay. And Daniel was in the water. I saw him. So were a couple of Tony's employees. I've seen them at the shop before, but I don't know their names. If you showed me a picture, I would recognize them, though. And Vesper. It's hard to miss her with the prosthetic leg. I saw Daniel's husband, Tom, paddle out at one point as well. But he was one of the organizers, and I'm pretty sure he was just putting a marker out there."

"Anyone else?"

"There was one other woman who I think Tony

used to date. But I'm not sure. She's one of the ones who warned me about him before I donated the kidney. Umm, Sally? Sammy? Something like that. She was out there. Apart from that, the others I didn't know."

"Okay, thanks, Lily."

"Are… are you close to finding out who killed him?"

"I can't really say. The thing about private investigating is, in my experience, you can feel like you're a million miles from the truth, like you're still at square one, and then all of a sudden, everything falls into place, just like that."

"I can understand that. But this is your way of telling me you feel as if you're nowhere."

"I wouldn't say nowhere. I'm not leaning in any one direction right now. But when I do find the killer, things will come to a head pretty quickly. When I know where to look, that's when it becomes easier to find the evidence needed to put someone behind bars."

"I hope it's quick. I really do. Tony didn't deserve this, and whoever killed him needs to be punished for it. Thank you for looking. I know you're doing it for your friend and that there's a chance she's the killer, but I still want to thank you. Because right now, I will take all the help I can get. The more people who care, who are looking for the killer, the better the odds of finding them, right?"

I nodded. "Absolutely."

I spoke with Lily for a couple more minutes then headed back to Queenie to find a message from Dot. We were meeting with the building manager to look at the available apartment in Rosie's building in just over an hour.

Chapter 15

I could count on one hand the number of times I'd been to Rosie's address, and I wasn't sure I'd ever actually been inside the building. The woman took her privacy seriously.

On the way, I stopped at Dot's place, and the two of us hopped into her car, thinking it would be less conspicuous than Queenie, especially if we had to come back and stake the place out. Dot emerged looking as if she'd just returned from her aerobic walking class, wearing a pastel-pink velour tracksuit and enormous, expensive-looking sunglasses, carrying a large designer straw tote.

"I don't know what look you're going for, but it's definitely giving off 'Betty White in *Golden Girls* marries a guy for his money and is now living the life after he's conked it' vibes," I said as I climbed into the driver's seat.

"Good. That's exactly what I'm going for. I'm not Dot anymore. I'm now Francine Murphy, recently widowed wife of Eugene Murphy. We're from Chicago originally, but we lived in Battle Creek, Michigan, for decades, where my husband worked for General Mills, and that's where he made his fortune. Eugene came up with the idea for Lucky Charms."

"I guess I owe my childhood to your fake husband, then."

"So you do. Eugene—may God rest his soul— was deathly afraid of flying. If only he'd been just as afraid of a brain aneurysm. So we never travelled, but now that he's passed, I've decided I'm going to be spending my winters somewhere far warmer than Michigan and Illinois, so I'm thinking about renting a place up here in Hawaii. I don't want to buy a property, as I'm a miser who won't want to leave it to my children, because they're all ingrates."

I snorted. "Sounds about right."

"But you, you're my granddaughter, the only good one of the bunch."

"Have I got a name?" I asked. I started the car and began driving.

"Melissa."

I scrunched up my face. "I have nothing against the name, but I don't look like a Melissa."

"Fine. What name do you want, then?"

"I want to be Taylor."

"Okay, fine. You're Taylor Murphy, and you're my granddaughter. You're the only one who has realized that I've left all my children out of the will, and you're taking advantage by taking care of your grandmother in the hopes that I'll leave everything to you. But I also realize that you're a gold-digger who doesn't actually care about her grandmother, and while I'm leading you on, pretending that you're going to be left in the will, in reality, I'm going to be leaving you with nothing."

"Wow, Taylor is offended," I replied. "You've put a lot of thought into this fake identity."

"We have to get our story straight. Besides, I was frustrated over that stupid camera."

"Can't find anything identifying?"

"No. I need the device the camera was connected to. It's the only way I'm going to be able to find the person who left it. That's what Rosie's doing now—she's checking out the place."

"Well, if Jake's around, Rosie won't get caught, at least. We can hope she finds whatever device that is."

"I agree. And in the meantime, Francine and Taylor Murphy have to find a suitable apartment and maybe uncover the identity of the thief in the complex."

"Exactly."

We arrived at Rosie's building after about five minutes and parked in one of the visitor's spots ten minutes before our scheduled meeting. The building was one of those nineties specials with three stories of rendered pink brick on the outside, a green roof, and white railings on the balconies. The outside of the building was surrounded by parking spots, and the complex obviously saved on landscaping by ensuring most of the property was concrete rather than plant based. However, on the outside of the lot, facing the street, large bushes had been put up to offer a bit of privacy to the residents.

"So, do we have a plan other than checking out this empty apartment? Are we just seeing if anyone feels suspicious? Talking to anyone we come across?" I asked.

Dot nodded. "Yes. Rosie also gave me the apartment numbers of a few people she thinks might be more likely to be the thief than others."

"Oh?"

Dot pulled a small notebook from her bag and started reading. "In apartment number 4, there's a man named Samuel Dodds. Rosie thinks he's dealing drugs."

"And if Rosie thinks that, it means he's dealing drugs."

"Exactly. She says one of his biggest customers is the guy in apartment number 12, on the second floor, named John."

"Okay. So we're thinking Samuel might be very

into getting a bit of extra quick cash, and John might *need* some quick cash."

"Yup. She's also said that the woman in apartment 15 has been acting strangely and bringing in large bags late at night for the past few weeks, but she doesn't know what that's about and hasn't had the time to investigate."

"You know, Rosie is living up to the stereotype of the nosy old lady who spies on her neighbors," I said with a laugh.

"She sure is. I had no idea about any of this. Those are the people she thinks are the most likely to be the thief, but she wants to stress that we keep an open mind."

"Okay. We will. Let's do this."

Dot and I got out of the car and headed toward the entrance to the building. Sure enough, it was as Rosie had said. A small black pad with a red light above it was next to the door handle. Beside it on the wall was a list of residents. I snapped a quick photo of it with my phone, and Dot did the same before pressing the button for apartment number 1, that of the on-site caretaker.

"Hello?" a gruff voice on the other end replied.

"Hi, this is Taylor Murphy, here with my grandmother," I replied chirpily. "We're here to look at the apartment for rent."

"I'll be out there in a second," the voice on the other end replied.

About a minute later, a man shuffled over to the front entrance and opened the door for us. He looked to be in his forties, with graying brown hair sitting like a mop on his head, wearing a pair of stained and faded jeans and a gray t-shirt that didn't fit him quite right. He carried a few extra pounds, and he moved slowly, as if he was constantly pushing through an invisible puddle of molasses.

"I'm Gareth, the manager here," he said, holding out a hand, which I reached forward and shook. Gareth's smile was friendly, hidden behind a somewhat unkempt beard that matched his graying hair.

"Taylor. And this is Francine, my grandmother."

"It's nice to meet you," Dot replied. She had switched to having a somewhat haughty air about her, sticking her chin out slightly. "This is the property, then? I was rather hoping it would be something a little bit more impressive from the outside, given the price range."

"Well, this isn't Michigan," Gareth replied as we entered. The main lobby was plain but well kept up, with a few upholstered chairs around a coffee table for anybody waiting and mailboxes against the wall at the far end. "Things are going to be more expensive than you're used to over here."

"That's all right, dear," Dot replied. "I never thought this would be a cheap decision, moving to Hawaii. But of course, I have to prioritize myself. I know I have a number of people in my family who don't care in the least about me, and they'll be happiest if I don't spend a penny of what I've got left, but now that my dear, sweet Eugene has passed, he would have wanted me to spend some of the money we worked so hard for."

"Yes, of course. I'm sorry for your loss," Gareth replied.

"Thank you. He was wonderful, Eugene. Did you know he came up with the idea for Lucky Charms? They're magically delicious, and so was he."

I bit back a smile as Gareth looked a little taken aback. "I had no idea."

"He was a genius, my Eugene. That was what I loved most about him."

"Why don't you tell us a bit about this property?" I chimed in. "I see it's near the water, which is good. Grandma loves the water, and this is a bit different from Lake Michigan, especially in February."

"Yes, it's very convenient. There's a small beach just at the end of the road, about two hundred feet from your front door. And if you go north a few blocks, you'll find yourself at the south end of Kalama Park, one of the biggest and best parks in town. This is a nice, quiet part of Kihei as well. We're almost halfway between north and south, so it's close to everything but without feeling like it's part of the action where all the young people are."

"Good," Dot replied with a nod.

"And at the same time, there's a mall with a grocery store and most things you'd need only a few minutes away. Will you be driving?"

"I'm thinking of moving here with her, to help take care of her," I interrupted quickly. After all, Taylor was supposed to be after the money. "I love my grandmother, and if I have to move across the country to help, I will. I would be getting a car. I would think I'd need one to help her get groceries."

Dot pursed her lips. "We will discuss it. But having a grocery store nearby is convenient all the same. I could always simply order a taxi."

"You could," Gareth said.

I narrowed my eyes at him.

"How is this complex in terms of safety? Obviously, with my grandmother not being as spry as she used to be, she's worried about that."

"We're a very secure complex, and we haven't had a single issue in years," Gareth lied smoothly. "You may have seen on the way in, we use an electronic key fob system for residents to enter the building. They're installed at all of the entrances in this complex, making it impossible for someone who doesn't have one to enter."

I saw Dot roll her eyes slightly behind Gareth's back. Obviously, what Dot considered impossible and what Gareth considered impossible were two very different things.

"Now, this is the apartment we've got for rent. Number 5. Please, feel free to have a look inside."

We walked in, and I started wondering how we were going to speak to anybody.

"Are you sure there haven't been any problems?" I asked. "I overheard a woman who lives here speaking with a friend at the grocery store the other day, and I asked them about their time here. They said it was great, other than the thief. What thief?"

Gareth sighed. "It's nothing, really. A temporary annoyance. Somebody in this complex has been taking advantage of people leaving their doors unlocked during the day and stealing small items. But they're going to be caught, and there's been nothing violent."

"All the same," Dot said, sounding horrified. "That's terrible."

"It is, and I'm working to find out who the responsible party is," Gareth replied. "I'm working with the owners, and I'm confident that whoever it is will be found soon."

"Do you have security cameras installed?" I asked.

"Not yet. It has never been in the budget, nor has it ever been necessary before. And I don't believe it is now, either. These are isolated incidents, and I promise you, so long as you lock your front door when you leave, you have nothing to worry about."

"All right, well, that is interesting. Although I must say, when it comes to the people near me stealing my fortune, I don't worry so much about strangers," Dot said. "I'm more concerned about the people closer to me."

I was getting frustrated. While Dot and I were doing our best, we were stuck inside this little apartment, and we had no way to get any information or to ask anybody else around here what might be going on.

After a little while, Dot asked Gareth to check on something in the bathroom for her and pulled me aside. "We need to do something here."

"I couldn't agree more."

"When we leave, I'm going to pull the fire alarm. I'll meet with residents outside, and you break into the apartments I gave you and see if you can find the stolen items."

I nodded. "Sounds like a plan."

A few seconds later, Gareth emerged from the bathroom. "No, I don't see the leak you're talking about at all, sorry. I'll come by again later and check to be sure."

"Well, it's no matter. I'm sure it's nothing. Thank you so much for your help today, Gareth. I think we've seen everything we need to."

"You're very welcome. We do have the application form online for you to fill out."

"Taylor can find that for me, can't you, dear?"

"Of course, Grandma," I replied with a smile.

Dot shuffled toward the door, and Gareth locked up after us. As we headed down the hallway back toward the main entrance, Dot grabbed one of the fire alarms and yanked.

Immediately, the ringing of the alarm rang through the hall. Dot let out a small shout and covered her ears. "What is that?" she asked.

"Fire alarm," Gareth replied. "Come with me to the exit, and then I have to help evacuate the building."

Gareth led us to the front door and then turned and rushed back inside. Dot left, flashing me a wink, and I followed Gareth as the residents began slowly trickling out.

Chapter 16

First up was Samuel's apartment, where Rosie was pretty sure he was dealing. I pulled out a small lockpicking kit from my purse. Rosie was still much better at this than I was, but I was coming along nicely, and less than thirty seconds later, I heard the click of the lock.

I was careful as I opened the door, not wanting to surprise Samuel if he happened to have decided to stay inside when he heard the alarm. But I didn't have to worry; it quickly became obvious the apartment was empty.

I moved quickly. I probably had ten, maybe fifteen minutes if I was lucky, to check the three apartments Rosie had listed. Samuel wasn't exactly subtle about his business. On the coffee table in the middle of the living room were a handful of Ziploc bags filled with a green substance I was pretty sure wasn't powdered oregano. Next to those were smaller baggies filled with what was obviously cocaine, but that wasn't my problem right now.

My eyes scanned the room, but I came up with no evidence that the stolen items were here. I headed to the bedroom and did a quick search as well but found nothing. I didn't think Samuel was the thief. If he was okay with leaving a bunch of coke and pot just lying around on the coffee table, he probably wouldn't be too fussed about hiding the proceeds of his other crimes, either.

I decided to move on. Next, I sprinted up the stairs to apartment 12. Picking that lock as well, I opened the door to find myself staring directly at a man sitting on the couch in the living room.

"Whoops, wrong apartment," I said cheerfully over the sound of the fire alarm, which was still beeping away.

"All good, bra. I've done that a few times," the man replied slowly. He looked to be in his early twenties, wearing a pair of board shorts and an oversized T-shirt on his thin frame, and going by the redness in his eyes and his thousand-yard-stare, this guy was higher than a BASE jumper getting ready to launch off the Burj Khalifa.

"You John?" I asked.

"I might be." I wasn't sure if he was trying to be mysterious or if he had genuinely forgotten his own name.

"Cool. Look, John, I'm trying to find some stuff that's been lost. Jewelry. You wouldn't happen to know anything about that, would you?"

"Jewelry? Like, gold shit? Nah. Haven't seen anything like that at all. I think I heard something like that, though."

"Do you mind if I have a quick look around just to be sure? It's important."

"Go for it."

There was no better outcome when you were caught breaking into someone's home than having that person invite you to look around.

"Did you find anything?" John asked when I was finished a couple minutes later.

"Nope. You're all clear."

"Too bad. I could use some bling."

"You haven't gone visiting someone else's apartment and taken any recently, have you?"

"Nah. Not my thing. I keep to myself. Chill vibes."

"Okay, well, have fun," I said.

"Bye," John said lazily as I stepped back out into the hall. On the bright side, if he even remembered I had actually been there and didn't just chalk it up to a stoner dream, he obviously didn't care.

I moved on to apartment 15. The alarm was still going, which was good. As soon as it stopped, I had to get out of here. I probably only had a minute or two left.

I worked on the lock to apartment 15, the one occupied by the woman bringing mysterious bags up to her apartment at night. It clicked open a few seconds later, and I entered cautiously, not wanting to get caught by someone doing fewer drugs than John but who might also have stayed inside during the alarm.

But as soon as I looked into the apartment, my mouth dropped. I wasn't sure what I had been expecting, but it wasn't pineapples.

Seriously, floor to ceiling. Pineapples everywhere. I walked inside, mouth open, gazing at the sight, trying to figure out if maybe I'd accidentally gotten high at John's place. Because seriously? They weren't even in crates or anything. At most, they were in reusable shopping bags. Every single piece of furniture had pineapples on it. The couch was completely covered except for one tiny little space, where I assumed the woman who lived here sat when they wanted to relax for a bit. But the bookshelves? Pineapples. The mantel? Pineapples. The TV stand? Pineapples.

I continued on into the kitchen to find piles and piles of empty mason jars. And more pineapples.

There had to be a thousand of them here at the very least.

Suddenly, the alarm stopped. It had been going on for so long, and my body had gotten so used to it, that the silence felt strange, and I could almost hear the beeping continuing inside my head. But no, it was gone, which meant that within a couple of minutes, the person who lived here would be coming back into their home.

I ran through what felt like the most tropical maze of all time, past all the pineapples, but that was all I found. Whole fruits filled every single inch of this apartment. Whatever was going on here was weird as hell, no question about that, but as far as I could tell, it had nothing to do with the recent thefts.

On my way out, my eyes landed on a single sheet of labels, and there was a social media username.

@pineapplefairydrink

I was going to have to check it out. But not now. When I was safely out of here. Although, just for good measure, I did grab a single pineapple and shoved it into my tote bag.

I quickly bailed and headed outside via one of the side exits just as people were returning to their homes.

I found Dot outside, and the two of us went back to her car. She hopped into the driver's seat and pulled out onto the street.

"Did you find anything?" she asked.

"One stoner, a whole lot of pineapples, and absolutely no jewelry," I said. "How about you?

Find anything interesting while you were out there talking to people?"

"Not much. I found out about the couple that lived in the apartment we looked at. I was interested. I thought maybe they had bailed on bad terms and were coming back to steal from people. After all, it wouldn't be difficult to get an extra key fob made up and not hand it back."

"But no?"

"No, they left about six weeks ago. He got a job on the mainland, so they're long gone."

"It was just two of them?"

"And a cat. Although one person swears they saw the cat about three weeks ago, but she also wore glasses so thick you could core them out and use them as soup cans."

"Well, I found something even more interesting: pineapples. That's what was in the third apartment, what Rosie saw that person bringing in at night."

"Pineapples? That's it? Just pineapples? It wasn't totally filled with drugs or anything, was it?"

"I don't think so. But just in case, I took one. We can have a look at it in case they're hiding something weird in them. And I found a social media username, too."

"What was it?"

"@pineapplefairydrink," I replied.

Dot pulled out her phone and punched that in.

A second later, a popular, trending TikTok song with a fun beat started playing over the speakers.

"It's a small business," Dot explained. "She's making pineapple drink and shipping it across the country, apparently."

"Haven't people learned their lesson after all the other times individuals decided to mail perishable food and it ended up being a horrible idea? The pink sauce was a disaster in every way," I said.

"Hey, it's pretty. Although I think you're right about the whole safety side of things. She's obviously doing this in her kitchen. And she's adding glitter to the drink."

"Glitter? Seriously?"

"Red and pink glitter, to imitate Maui's beautiful sunrises, according to the caption," Dot read.

I pulled the car over. "Okay, I need to see this." Grabbing the phone from Dot, I watched as the video started again.

Sure enough, this was definitely being filmed in the kitchen I had been standing in a few minutes earlier. The woman had a mason jar out and a pineapple next to it. Then the video cut away, and all the pineapple had magically been cut into chunks. Another cut, and the chunks had been turned into juice.

"Drink the magic of the tropics with the freshest pineapple you can get," came over the top of the video. "Straight from Maui, but from a small organic farm, not a mega-corp with questionable worker practices."

"I mean, I'm on board with small businesses," I said.

"Me too, but wait until she adds the glitter."

Then, sure enough, into frame came a couple of jars of glitter. I knew edible glitter existed. I was a thirty-year-old woman with an Instagram account and a penchant for buying gimmicky vodka online. Every summer, edible glitter one could add to drinks was basically the only thing I saw ads for. But I was pretty sure this was the kind of glitter you got in bulk-size containers at Michael's.

"She's going to add this to the drink," I whispered almost in horror. Sure enough, a perfectly manicured hand entered the frame and scooped out a teaspoon of pink glitter and a teaspoon of red glitter and added them to the mason jar.

"You don't just deserve a drink that will make you feel good, you deserve a drink that will look good while you're enjoying it," a text pop-up read. "Feel like you're experiencing a Maui sunset while you enjoy your pineapple fairy drink, straight from the island itself."

"It's about to get worse," Dot said.

"No. How is it going to be worse? It can't be worse. She just added glitter. Anyone who drinks this is going to make their toilet look like a nineties rave for weeks."

Dot snorted. "Keep watching."

My eyes were glued to the screen as if it featured a train wreck I couldn't look away from. Another text bubble appeared. "But it's not a Maui sunset without the famous honu, is it?"

Then, the camera switched to a giant box, and I gasped. "I recognize these! They're from the nineties," I exclaimed. When I was a kid, little balls filled with oil that melted in hot water had been the greatest thing you could ever possibly add to your bath. And they came in shapes. Like turtles. "She's not going to add them to the drinks, is she?"

I watched in horror as sure enough, the perfectly manicured hands grabbed three or four of the little balls and the turtles and dropped them into the mason jar.

"These are filled with healthy fats to negate the effects of the carbs and natural sugars found in the juice" a caption said.

"No. No, no, no. I refuse to believe people are buying this," I said. But I looked at the corner of the video and saw two million likes. Plus there was the fact that the apartment was filled to the brim with pineapples. This was selling. And it was selling well.

I opened up the comments, thinking that surely, a majority of people were going to agree with me. There had to be people on that app who were old enough to recognize the oil-filled capsules going into the drinks were actually bath accessories from twenty years ago. Right?

Wrong.

This drink is genius. I ordered it as soon as I heard about it a few weeks ago, and it helps me feel like a queen in the morning. Plus, it's so healthy! I love the oils you can add to make it into a balanced meal.

"A balanced meal?" I said, turning to Dot. "What is this world coming to? And this is coming from someone who ate pie for breakfast this morning and hasn't had anything to eat since."

Dot laughed. "That's the thing about the internet. What used to be a weird fad in your small town was limited to there. Now, these things can become global."

Amanda sent me five jars, and I'm hooked. Every morning, when I drink these, I feel like I'm in the tropics. I'm not a big fan of the oil, as I'm currently on a low-fat diet, but they look beautiful.

"Okay, maybe, just *maybe* the oil is food safe," I said, trying to reason this out before my brain exploded. "Maybe she got it custom made."

"Do you really believe that?" Dot asked.

"No. And I will admit, drinking one or two of those oil things won't permanently ruin your life."

Dot raised an eyebrow at me. "Youthful indiscretion?"

"That's a nice thing to call the complete and total lack of common sense I had as a seven-year-old," I replied with a smile. "I'm pretty sure I'm part of the reason there are safety warnings on labels now."

Dot laughed. "Well, I'm glad you made it through your ordeal."

"The worst part is, the oil wasn't actually *that* bad. I bet it would have been somewhat decent if added to juice. But I wasn't thinking I was drinking it as some sort of healthy morning smoothie. This is wild."

"It's the internet. In many ways, it's still the Wild West. When you think about it, the internet has only been readily accessible to the majority of the population for about twenty-five years, tops. That's one generation. I was an adult when I learned of its existence already. In the whole scope of human industry, that's nothing."

"You're right," I agreed.

"So there are going to be mistakes made. There are going to be rapid changes as people learn how to function in this new world. And that means scams, because that's how humanity functions. There have always been scams. There's a tablet from ancient Mesopotamia that was taken from the Sumerian city of Ur to the British museum, in which a man complains about the quality of copper he was sold by a merchant named Ea-Nasir."

"Hey, I saw those memes," I said with a grin.

"Exactly. Even then, thousands of years ago,

there was a man scamming others by selling low-quality copper. The only thing that's different now is the reach the internet offers. If people didn't learn their lesson about buying food from unlicensed individuals on the internet before, maybe they'll learn it now."

"I hope so. I can't believe she's got millions of likes on that account. And it's all going to go awry when people find out that she's running a giant pineapple juice mill out of a one-bedroom apartment. But on the bright side, I don't think she's the thief. There was no sign of the jewelry, and I think she's got her hands full at the moment anyway. Or her pineapples full. The frustrating thing is, apart from that, I didn't learn anything that might help us."

"There was no sign of the jewelry in the other apartments?"

"No, and the way Sam leaves his drugs just hanging around in plain sight, I don't think he would have bothered with sticking the jewelry somewhere hidden, either. And John, the stoner, was still in his apartment. I think he actually would have told me where the loot was if he'd done it."

"Hmm. Rosie has checked the local pawn shops too. I know that. She would have seen the items there if they'd been hawked."

"Yeah, but with things like Facebook Marketplace these days, it's very easy to create a fake account and sell anything there," I pointed out. "Or even Craigslist."

"Also true."

"So all we've done is rule out three apartments from the fifty-odd in that complex. I mean, it's not nothing, but it doesn't feel like we're especially close to finding the thief."

"I agree," Dot said. "We need to do a proper stakeout, but how are we going to get a look at those hallways without anyone noticing? We could go the tiny-camera route, the way whoever was black-mailing Tony did, but Rosie says she doesn't want to do that."

I frowned. "In that case, we have to do it old school. Sit in the car, watch the windows, and hoping we see someone who doesn't belong walk into an apartment. I just wish this was one of the buildings with only one side that faces outward."

"That might be what it comes down to," Dot said. "But for now, change of plans. We have to get to the airport. I got a notification. Brady Ludlam, a Ham brothers associate, is arriving in about forty minutes."

I nodded, fighting the sinking feeling in my stomach. I really hoped this was just going to be another Seattle gangster going on vacation.

Chapter 17

Dot and I drove straight to the airport from Rosie's apartment building. We received a text from her that she was finished in Paia and would meet us at Dot's apartment.

"So who is this guy?" I asked as we pulled out onto the highway. "High up in the organization?"

"Just high enough that he's the sort of guy the Ham brothers would trust to do something like this but without being one of their second-in-command-level guys. They might be trying to lay low. Brady went to high school with Stevie, which is how he got introduced to the gang."

"Oh, good, so he'll have been friends with the guy I shot. That means he won't want any revenge at all," I deadpanned.

"We always knew this was a risk. Now, if this

turns out to be what we think it is, we'll have to deal with it. But we can't turn back the clock."

"I know. But that doesn't mean I can't be upset at the situation."

"That is true."

"And if he has come here to kill me, I'm going to make Tony's death look like he passed away peacefully in his sleep," I muttered. "I never wanted to kill Stevie. I had just been trying to get through my shift and get paid. It wasn't my fault he robbed me at gunpoint. I was trying to save my own life. And now this. It never ends. It's like I'm being constantly punished for something somebody else did."

Dot reached over from the steering wheel and placed a hand over mine. "I know. It's never a good feeling when something you were forced into comes back and has consequences on your future. You feel like you're trapped and like you're never going to be truly free. But that time will come. You will have the opportunity to break from the cage. And this might be the beginning of that. Look at it that way. But we're playing the long game here. We're not going to barge into baggage claim, guns blazing."

"The TSA might not be big fans of us if we did, either."

"Exactly. We're going to do this smart. We're going to follow Brady, and we're going to see what he does. And then, if he comes after you, we're going to destroy him," she said as simply as if she were listing what groceries she needed to grab before heading home.

We pulled into the parking lot at Kahului about five minutes after the daily Alaska Airlines flight from Seattle had landed. Heading to baggage claim, Dot pulled out her phone and showed me a photo of the man we were looking for.

Brady Ludlam was in his mid-twenties, with short, spiked, platinum-blond hair that would have been fashionable if it were still 2002. His dark eyes were empty, as if there was nothing going on inside that head. His large mouth scowled into the camera, and he had a square chin with a large crease in the middle.

"He's five foot eleven, according to his file with the Seattle PD," Dot said.

I looked around the baggage claim area. Kahului airport was honestly due for a pretty big upgrade. This airport looked like it hadn't been renovated since at least the eighties. But I wasn't here to complain about how this building was painted in colors more suited to a military base than the first impression tourists got when they landed on the island. I was here to find Brady.

It didn't take long before I spotted him. I elbowed Dot gently and motioned with my chin toward him as he emerged through the doors to baggage claim. "That's him, right?"

"Sure is," Dot agreed. "Let's follow him."

Brady didn't have checked baggage, just a carry-on duffel bag which he slung over his shoulder as he walked out of the arrivals area and toward the large building where most of the top-tier car rental companies were located.

"He's going to Thrifty," I said, watching as he entered.

Dot nodded.

The two of us headed back to the parking lot. This time, I took the keys. I pulled Dot's car over to where we could see the cars leaving the rental area. Twenty minutes later, I spotted him.

"That's him," I said, pulling out behind a flashy red Mustang. Apparently, Brady was going all-out.

"That's not a great car if he wants to be spying on you and be subtle about it," Dot said.

"This guy doesn't strike me as being a big thinker," I replied.

Suddenly, music began thumping from his stereo system. "Is that... is that the Vengaboys?" I asked, rolling down my window to hear better. Sure enough, I knew that song. It had been all the rage back when I was in sixth grade.

Dot grinned. "I bet he's taking advantage of being away from all his buddies to listen to what he *really* likes."

"Honestly, this song is a banger. He could have worse taste."

"I've always been more into hard rock than pop. The eighties were a good time for my taste in music."

"All big hair and tight pants?"

"Absolutely. I won't say music was better then, because I know people are allowed to like whatever they want, but that's my era of choice."

"I like most music styles. Except country. But everything else is fair game. I think my Spotify Wrapped has a little bit of a cry every year when it has to try and put a label on what I listen to."

"That's good too. Always keep 'em guessing."

"Exactly. Taylor Swift, followed by Wu Tang Clan. Then an old-school Bon Jovi song to round it all out."

"I'm with you on the Bon Jovi."

"There you go," I said with a grin. "Anyway, I'll bop along to this with Brady, but I don't want to draw suspicion to us. If he's here to spy on me, we don't want him noticing that we've already got eyes on him. If we're lucky, he's going to take the turn-off to go to Ka'anapali and hang out on the beach and drink mai tais for a week."

Unfortunately, when we got to the main inter-section, Brady continued going straight. He got onto the Piilani Highway running behind Kihei, and when he finally turned off, my blood turned to ice.

"You don't have to say it," Dot said quietly. This

was the turnoff I took to get back to my apartment. And sure enough, Brady drove past it slowly.

I wanted to throw up.

"That's not a coincidence," I said. "That's not a guy trying to find his hotel and getting lost. That's someone who was given my address and is staking out the place."

Dot nodded. "You're right. Sorry, Charlie. I know you were hoping he was just here on vacation. Hell, so was I. This isn't what either one of us wanted."

"Yeah. And there's no point in burying our heads in the sand, either. This is happening. They're here, and they've found me somehow. I need to let Zoe know."

Dot nodded. "Absolutely."

"And Jake. This is a real threat."

"Yes. Although I don't think it'll be immediate. I might be wrong, but I think they're just scoping things out for now."

"I agree."

We followed Brady as he continued along the street then turned onto South Kihei Road. About half a mile down the road, he turned off into one of those big blocks full of apartments being rented out as Airbnbs.

"This must be where he's staying," I said, cruising on past so as to not draw suspicion.

Dot nodded. "I'll see what I can find out. Places

like that, they have extra security. If they have cameras, I might be able to get access to those. We'll keep an eye on him."

"Thanks."

The two of us drove back to Dot's place in silence. I was lost in my thoughts. After all this time, I had thought I might have been safe. But the reality was that the Ham brothers had found me. And they were going to want revenge for their brother's death, even though it was his fault he was dead. I hadn't asked him to rob me. I had told him to stop. I had told him I would shoot if he tried to come after me, and he still had.

I didn't want to kill him. I just wanted to get through my shift without dying.

As we pulled into Dot's apartment complex, I realized I was clutching the steering wheel so hard my knuckles had turned white.

Dot turned to me. "Look at me, Charlie."

I did as she asked.

"We're going to stop them. Your life isn't going to be ruined by this. Whatever the Ham gang is planning, we're going to foil it. You got me?"

I took a deep breath. "I do. Thanks, Dot."

"I was never the type to have kids, but if I had, I could have only dreamed that they would turn out to be as much of a badass as you are. You're strong enough to take these guys on, and you have a whole group of friends who are willing to help. And this old dog still knows a few tricks," Dot added with a wink.

"There's no one I'd rather have by my side right now than you and Rosie," I said. "Thanks, Dot. I really appreciate it."

The two of us headed upstairs to meet Rosie, who I hoped had had more luck today than we had.

Chapter 18

"So how did it go?" Dot asked as soon as we walked into the apartment. Rosie had made herself at home and was busy reading the local paper at the kitchen table.

"Not well, unfortunately. I had a very good look at the home. And a dozen houses also within that three-hundred-foot radius we thought the camera could potentially reach. Nothing. Not a single sign that there had been a phone or laptop or iPad or anything else that could have streamed the data from the camera in Tony's house."

"So they obviously got there and got rid of all the evidence they could," I said. "It would make sense that they would have done it after Tony's death. With the police snooping around, the black-mailer wouldn't have dared to enter the house and get the camera."

"Right. Not everyone is as crazy as we are," Dot said with a grin.

I laughed. "There is that. But also, even more so if they're the killer. They wouldn't want to get caught. But they did think to get rid of the device the camera was streaming to. Does that mean you're out of leads, Dot?"

"I think so. I don't believe there's any way of tracking down who that camera belonged to without having access to the device it was streaming to."

"Okay, so I think we can summarize today as being a giant disaster on all counts. We didn't find out who the thief in your building is, either. However, I can confirm that Samuel is dealing drugs, that John is almost certainly one of his customers, and the person who was bringing in large bags of a mysterious item is running a business on TikTok and Instagram selling definitely-not-approved-for-human-consumption juice made with pineapple, glitter, and oil."

"Well, that's certainly not what I expected," Rosie said, shaking her head.

"It was a surprise to me too," I replied. "But I don't think she's the one stealing. I didn't see any sign of the jewelry. Besides, she's obviously got her hands full with ten thousand orders of gross juice the internet has fallen in love with."

"Until the first time it gives someone botulism," Dot muttered.

"Well, yeah. But ultimately, then, today was a waste. We got no closer to finding the killer, and we got no closer to finding the thief, either. Tomorrow, when Tony's business opens up for the day, I'm going to go speak to Daniel again. I think he might have something to do with this. He obviously wasn't entirely honest with me when we spoke on the beach."

"Good thinking," Rosie said.

"Oh, Rosie, you should also know that Brady Ludlam is coming after me," I said. "He arrived this afternoon, and we followed him out of the airport. He drove slowly past my place before going to his."

Rosie nodded. "I thought that would be the case. I am sorry, Charlie."

"Thank you. We're going to have to follow him."

"I will take care of that," Rosie said. "Charlie, at the moment, you can't let him know we're onto him. He has no idea who Dot and I are, and I can watch him without being seen myself. You need to live life normally, and we'll see what happens. If he tries anything, he'll regret it."

"Thanks," I said gratefully. "I really appreciate it. I'm going to being Zoe and Jake in the loop, too. They both deserve to know what's going on."

"That is smart, I think," Rosie said.

"Okay. I'll head off now," I said. "I'll see you later."

I left Dot's apartment, and as I walked toward Queenie, I pulled out my phone and sent Jake a text.

Hey. I know you're balls to the wall right now, but I really have to talk to you. It's important, and it doesn't have to take long. I'll be at my apartment in about ten minutes, if you can just pop by then.

I hopped into the Jeep and drove back to the apartment.

When I returned, however, I saw a sight I wasn't expecting. In the parking lot, a police car's red-and-blue lights flashed, the colors casting dancing shadows and blasting light on the walls, trees, and other landscaping like the world's most depressing Broadway production. In the windows, I could see faces peering out, trying to see what was going on.

Good question. I wanted to know too. I headed to the front door just in time to see Jake and Liam coming out with Vesper between them, handcuffed.

"Vesper!" I shouted, running toward her.

"It's all good, babe. Don't you worry about me. I'm not saying shit without a lawyer. I know better than that."

"Come on," Liam snarled at her. "Just because you've only got one leg doesn't mean you can't move."

"Liam," Jake snapped at his partner.

"You've only got one brain cell, but I don't complain about you being too dumb to string two coherent thoughts together," Vesper snapped back at him. "So maybe let's lay off the insults based on disability, because you're at an automatic disadvantage."

I let out a snort, and Liam glared at her.

"Don't talk to them," I called out. "I'll get Zoe's mom to meet you. Jake, where are you taking her?"

"Kihei Police Station," Jake replied.

"This is wrong. She didn't do this," I said.

"I can't talk to you about an open police investigation," Jake replied. "Sorry. Now, let us do our job."

Jake and Liam pushed past, leading Vesper along. I could only stand and watch as she was led into the car. Jake looked at me one last time before he got into the driver's side, pausing for a second as if he wanted to say something. Then, he thought better of it, got in, and drove off.

I seethed with rage as I stormed into the building. How dare he arrest Vesper? She was innocent. I knew it. There was no way she would have killed Tony, and now she'd been taken away in front of the whole building. This was ridiculous.

I opened the door and slammed it behind me. Zoe, standing at the kitchen counter, raised her eyebrows. "I guess you saw what went on outside?"

"Yeah. It's bull."

"It might not be. We don't know. But I've called

my mom already. She's going to go down to the station."

"Good. Vesper needs a lawyer who can get her off. She didn't do this."

"Have you got proof?"

"No, but I doubt Jake does, either. And the only proof Liam recognizes is what's on his stupid Jim Beam bottle he drinks at the end of the night."

"Maybe they found something you don't know about," Zoe suggested. "Wait until my mom goes and sees Vesper. She'll find out what she can, and if Vesper gives her permission, she'll tell us what they know."

I paced around the room. "I hope so. I can't believe they actually arrested her."

"Have you found evidence it could be someone else?"

"Well, I know Tony's business wasn't doing well despite Daniel telling me the opposite of that. There were problems in his life that had nothing to do with his relationships. And he was being blackmailed. But no one wants to listen to that. It's so much easier to just blame the ex and move on."

"Blackmailed? Really?"

"Yup. And someone put at least one hidden camera in his house."

"Wow."

"And the police don't know about the camera. The only reason we found it was because of Rosie.

But the problem is, we can't trace it to anyone. But we need to."

"Because there's a good chance the blackmailer either is the murderer or knows perfectly well who might have a good motive," Zoe finished for me.

"Exactly. But we've hit a dead end. I've hit a dead end on everything, it feels like. But I have to keep pushing through, because now, Vesper's been arrested."

"What are you doing next?"

"Seeing Daniel tomorrow. The company wasn't doing nearly as well as he said it was. And I spoke to Lily today. She indicated that he and Tony might have been having disagreements about where to go with it from there. But she wasn't one hundred percent sure."

Zoe nodded. "You feel like Tony wasn't letting her in on his whole life?"

"No. I actually get the impression he was really trying. But the company was doing badly, and I don't think he wanted her to know exactly *how* badly, which I can't really blame him for. No one wants to admit to the person they love that their business is falling apart. He was putting a positive spin on it. Saying that they were aiming for fast growth. But from what Rosie and Dot were saying, they were investing money in sales but getting blocked up in production. It never would have worked. That's what I want to talk to Daniel about."

"Good thinking."

"But of course, now, with Vesper having been arrested, it's even more important to find the killer. Also, you should know: the gangsters in Seattle have found me. One of them landed this afternoon and drove slowly past this place. They know where I live. I would understand if you want to leave for a bit."

Zoe stared at me. "You're serious."

"Yeah."

"Oh, Charlie, I'm really sorry. I know it must be terrifying."

I paused for a second. "It's not great. I think the scariest part for me right now is not knowing what's going to happen next. Are they going to try and kill me? Just scare me? I think it's the former. They're gangsters, and I killed their brother. It's not like this is a gang known for taking it easy on people."

"No."

"Obviously, given your history with that stalker, I would understand if you decide to move out for a bit. Even if you hadn't been through that, I wouldn't blame you. These are gangsters. It's possible you're in danger just by being near me."

Zoe shook her head. "Not right now. You said it's one person, and he just drove slowly past this place?"

"Yeah."

"That's not enough to scare me off. And besides, I don't want you handling this by yourself. You helped me out when I had a stalker, so the least I can do is the same for you. I'm staying."

"Has anyone ever told you you're the best?"

"You, on a few occasions."

"Well, if you end up changing your mind, I would get it. Rosie and Dot are going to be keeping an eye on him for now, so I don't think he'll get to try anything."

"Good to know, though. I'll be careful. And you should be too."

"Definitely. Don't worry. I know these guys are bad news. I moved halfway across the Pacific Ocean to get away from them. They left a severed finger on my doorstep. I still don't know who it belonged to. I won't mess around."

"Have you told Jake?"

"I texted him, letting him know I needed to talk, but he hasn't replied yet. Too busy arresting our neighbor for a crime she didn't commit."

"Good. He'll keep an eye out too, for sure."

"Definitely. Listen, I'm going to go down there. I want to talk to him. And I'm pretty antsy, given everything that's just gone on."

"Okay. I'll talk to you later. Be careful, Charlie."

"I will," I promised.

Right now, Jake was going to be the one who had to be careful. He had just arrested my client, and I was sure he had virtually no evidence of her guilt.

Chapter 19

I drove to the police station with two aims: to let my boyfriend know about the potential threat to my life and to let him know about the potential threat to his if he kept my client in jail.

Seriously, what the hell? He couldn't have had any actual evidence of Vesper's guilt. This was ridiculous. I pulled into the Kihei police station and walked in through the front door. As soon as he looked up and saw me, Jake came over. I motioned for him to follow me outside.

"What are you doing here, Charlie?"

"I have to talk to you. Didn't you get my text?"

"Can it wait?"

"It kind of could, but now I also have to talk to you about Vesper."

"That can definitely wait."

"No, it can't."

"Charlie, I know she's your client, and I know you like her, but we have enough evidence she killed Tony to arrest her."

"And what evidence might that be?"

"I can't tell you that. It's police business."

"It's my business too."

"It's really not."

"Okay, then, I'm going to tell you the other thing, the reason I texted you. I've never told you why I moved back to Hawaii. But I'm going to tell you now. I was working at a jewelry store in Seattle when Stevie Ham, the brother of Connor and Braden, the infamous Ham brothers, decided to rob me. There was a bit of a kerfuffle, and he ended up shot. By me. I found a severed finger in a box at my front door a few days later, and I figured it was probably a good idea to get out of Dodge."

Jake's expression was inscrutable. "You know, if anybody else told me that story, I wouldn't believe them. Why wouldn't you tell me that before?"

"Because on top of it being traumatizing, I don't always feel like going around telling people that I killed the brother of two gang leaders in self-defense."

"I'm a detective. And your boyfriend."

"And I like to shove my feelings so deep down inside of me that they know what my first-ever meal was. I didn't tell you this before because it's my problem. But I'm telling you now."

"Because it might be becoming everyone's problem?"

"Yeah. A couple months back, Alicia got a phone call from someone in Seattle who was asking about me. I've been tracking everyone in the Ham gang since. Today, one of them landed at Kahului and drove past our apartment building. Slowly."

Jake ran a hand up and down his face. "So they're coming after you."

"I think it's safe to say that's the eventual goal."

"Let me get this straight: you killed a gangster in Seattle, ran to Hawaii to get away from them, and now they've found you."

"Yeah, that's pretty much it."

"I swear, sometimes, your life sounds like it's come right out of the plot of a movie."

"An Oscar-worthy one, I hope. And I want Margot Robbie to play me."

"Okay. Seriously, what do you need me to do? You're in trouble here."

"Nothing for now. I have Dot and Rosie keeping an eye on him."

"You do realize telling me you've got two women who could be your grandmothers keeping tabs on him is not reassuring."

"It should be. They won't lose him. They'll see what he's doing, and if something seems fishy, they'll take care of it. I promise. But I want you to know just in case."

"Right. With gang members, you never know what they're going to do next. And revenge for the brother you killed means they're going to go to any lengths to get that revenge."

"The worrying part is they're not coming in guns blazing. They're actually thinking things through, and they're spying on me. They're going to try and actually get away with my murder. Because that's what's going to happen. You don't leave a finger on someone's doorstep if you don't intend to kill them."

"I can't believe they did that," Jake said quietly.

"I got the message."

"Jesus, Charlie."

I thought Jake was about to start lecturing me, but instead, he pulled me in close, wrapped me in his arms like a comforting cocoon, and rested his head on top of mine.

"You're the strongest woman I've ever met."

I stood there awkwardly for a second, not entirely sure what to do. This was a different kind of hug. But slowly, I let my body relax, and I leaned into it, pressing my head against Jake's chest.

"I really hoped the past wasn't going to come back to haunt me," I admitted. "I just wanted to live my life in peace. Or at least the closest to peace I was ever going to get. I don't want them coming after me. I don't want them coming after the people I love."

Tears began to well in my eyes, but I blinked them back. I wasn't going to cry in front of Jake. I'd never cried in front of a boyfriend before, and I wasn't about to break that streak now.

"I know," he murmured. "And I'm sorry you're going through this. But if anyone can handle this, it's you. And you're not alone. You have me. You have those old ladies, who will do their best, but who I'm terrified for if I'm honest."

A strangled laugh leapt from my throat. "Oh, I don't think you have to worry too much about them."

"You've also got Zoe. And your mom."

"I know. And I'm terrified for them, too. If they do something…"

"They won't," Jake said firmly. "I won't let anything happen to you, Charlie. I promise."

I closed my eyes and leaned into his chest, letting myself relax for a few seconds. "Thanks, Jake. And if they try and do anything to you, I'm going to rip out their intestines while they're still alive and use them as nooses to hang them with their own colons."

"There's a thought you probably shouldn't say out loud within five hundred feet of a police station," he murmured.

"Speaking of, I'm not leaving here until I get to take Vesper home."

"In that case, you'd better get comfortable, because it's going to be twenty-five years."

I pulled away from Jake's hug. "You're joking. You can't have actual evidence. Come on. It's Vesper. She didn't do this. Whatever you think you've got, it's wrong."

"I'm not going to tell you what it is, but I promise you, it was enough to get an arrest warrant."

"You have to tell me. I'm her private investigator."

"That's not at all how the law works."

"You have to tell me because I'm your girlfriend."

"That's not at all how relationships work."

"I realize that's probably a good thing overall, but in this particular case, I want to know."

"And I want a pet llama that pukes up hundred-dollar bills on command, but sometimes, you just can't get what you want."

"Yeah, but yours is ridiculous. And why a llama?"

Jake shrugged. "Why not a llama? They're cool, and they spit at people they don't like."

"Fair enough. I wish I could do that without getting punched in the face too."

"So no, I'm not telling you why we arrested Vesper."

"I'm telling you, seriously, you have the wrong

person."

"Okay, who are you looking at?"

"For one thing, the person who was spying on Tony with miniature cameras."

Jake tried to hide it, but we were dating. I knew him well at this point. Well enough to see a teeny flicker of confusion flash across his face before he masked it once more.

"Aha! You don't know about the cameras. And yet you still think you've found the killer."

Jake pursed his lips. "Maybe I do know about the cameras."

"Nope," I said, shaking my head confidently. "You're trying to hide it, but you can't. I'm your girlfriend. You can't hide this stuff from me. You don't have a clue."

"You're impossible sometimes, you know that?" Jake replied, shooting me an unimpressed look. "Okay, fine. I don't know about a camera. What was going on with that?"

"You have to tell me I'm the best girlfriend in the world first," I sang.

"Sometimes, when I'm with you, I'm not sure if I want to laugh or cry."

"That's the nicest thing anyone's ever told me and exactly what I aim for in life. Okay, fine. You don't have to sing the song. But I am the best girlfriend ever, because I'm going to help you solve this case. There was a camera in Tony's home. At least one."

"Did you track it?"

I shook my head. "Nope. It was sending Bluetooth signals to another device, likely off the property, which we weren't able to recover. The trail went cold. Believe me, if it was possible to trace it to someone, we would have done it."

"The Maui Police have an entire IT department whose job it is to track these things down."

"My IT department is better," I said with a casual smile. "But you can have the camera. I'll give it to you to trace."

"So who's to say it wasn't Vesper?"

"You've obviously never had to help her unsubscribe from weird websites that she totally doesn't know how they got onto her computer and why they're charging her fees."

"Weird websites?" Jake asked, raising an eyebrow.

"She swore she would beat me to death with her prosthetic leg if I told anyone," I said, holding a hand to my heart while I bit back a couple of giggles. "But let's just say some people need to have their Apple Stylus taken away from them."

"I'm not sure I want to know any more."

"You definitely don't. Some of those images I've seen are imprinted on my brain forever. But Vesper can't do something like this. I love her, but she doesn't have the technical skills."

"We've been through Tony's emails. Personal and professional. And his phone. Whoever was doing this wasn't going through there."

"Or he was deleting the contents off the server. Or he had a secret email address. How about we trade: the camera for the hard drive on his computer."

"How about instead, you be a good citizen and just hand over the evidence of a possible crime to the police, and I don't give you evidence of a murder instead?"

"That's much less fun."

"It's also much more legal."

"Details."

"Details that get kicked out as evidence when we go to court. I can't let you have that hard drive."

"Fine. It was worth a shot."

"It really wasn't."

I narrowed my eyes at Jake. "Seriously, though. Someone who isn't Vesper was blackmailing Tony, someone who might be the same person but might be different was spying on her with a camera, and you arrested her without even knowing about it. That blackmailer, or the person with the camera, is a pretty good suspect, don't you think?"

Jake sighed. "Yes. I'll admit, we didn't know about that. How did you find the camera? You didn't go back to the house after I told you not to, did you?"

"I swear, I didn't. But I'm not willing to say more."

"Sometimes, I'm glad you decided to become a private investigator and not a criminal. As infuriating as you are, I think you'd be good at it."

"Aww, now *that's* the nicest thing you've ever said to me," I said with a smile, which earned me an exasperated look from Jake.

"You're impossible."

"You're the one not giving me what I want, despite me telling you all about a whole side of this case you didn't realize existed."

"Also, just because someone had a secret camera they used to spy on Tony doesn't mean they're the person who killed him."

"No. But arresting someone for his murder even though you don't have all the facts, because you didn't realize he was being spied on, is a little premature, don't you think?"

"The thing about murder is you're not always going to get *all* the facts. But we did have enough facts to arrest Vesper for the murder."

"And now?"

"Now, we do have a new avenue to go down before I'm willing to send this over to the DA for trial. I don't want Vesper to go to jail if she's innocent."

"So you're going to let her go?"

"That's not up to me," Jake said, shaking his

head. "If it were, I would say yes. At least temporarily. We obviously have a new lead we need to follow. I don't think Vesper is a flight risk, and I don't believe in keeping people in jail unnecessarily when they haven't been convicted of a crime yet."

"What happens now, then?"

"I'm going to bring up the camera thing to my captain. Let him know we may have screwed up and acted a bit prematurely. I'll get yelled at, but better that than to land an innocent person in jail."

"I'll get you the camera," I promised.

"Thanks. I wish you'd told me about this before. This is a murder investigation."

"You had an entire team go through that house. It's not like you didn't have the opportunity to find it before I did. And I've been telling you from the start that Vesper was innocent. It's not my fault you decided to act before you had all the facts. And I don't owe you what I've found, either. My investigation being better than yours doesn't mean you're automatically entitled to everything I've found, especially when it doesn't work the other way."

"You don't get it, do you?" Jake replied. "I *can't* just give you evidence to a crime. You have so many fewer rules to follow. And that's by design. We're the first line to getting justice for people. Without these rules, corruption in the police would be so much higher than it is now. I know you like to dance around the rules, but if I do it, it has real consequences. Like murderers getting away with their crimes. I know we're dating now, and I'm glad we are, but I'm not going to put my investigations at risk. I'm not going to put my job at risk just because we're together."

"I get it," I shot back. "I don't want you to lose a case or lose your job because of me. But I'm also not just some idiot off the street. I'm a private investigator, and we both have the same goal: to find the killer and bring them to justice. And yet every single time I bring it up, you're always doing your best to keep me as far away as you can, even though I've proven I'm not bad at this. It's more than just what's legal. You're pushing me away from your investigations, and it's not fair that I'm bringing you evidence and you stonewall me at every turn."

Before Jake had a chance to respond, the front door to the building opened, and Vesper walked out, followed closely by Zoe's mom, Julia Morgan.

Chapter 20

"Charlie, fancy meeting you here," Vesper said with a grin.

"You've been released?" Jake asked.

"No thanks to you. I did tell you I had the best lawyer in town and that to top it all off, I am innocent."

"Come on, Vesper. You know what I told you back there. No antagonizing the police, as much as you'd like to. We don't talk to them at all," Zoe's mom said.

"I have to go," Jake said, and he pushed past me and back into the police station. He wasn't happy. I knew that much. But I was right. I was offering to work with him, and at every turn, he was pushing me away. I forced the thought aside and turned to Vesper and Julia.

"What happened?" I asked.

Julia smiled. Zoe's mom was gorgeous. One of the best lawyers on the island, she was semiretired now but still took on the odd case when it suited her. Her blond hair was short, cut in a choppy bob that was styled to look professional. Her pants were navy blue, and she wore a pale-pink blouse. A brown leather messenger bag hung from her shoulder.

"It turns out the police didn't have nearly the amount of evidence they implied they did when they arrested my client," Julia said. "Charlie, it's nice to see you again. Vesper told me you're working this case on her behalf."

I nodded. "Yeah. It's crap that they think she killed Tony. I'm going to prove it."

"Good. Zoe told me you're becoming quite the skilled investigator."

"Thanks," I said with a grin.

I had always liked Julia. When I was a kid, most of the parents I knew had tried to calm me down. They wanted me to be more of the girls-should-be-seen-and-not-heard variety. But not Julia. She had always encouraged me to speak my mind, to follow my dreams, and to do whatever I wanted, no matter what anyone else thought of me. Having that kind of support from my best friend's mom was priceless to an eight-year-old.

"All right, ladies. I'm going to head off. Vesper, if the police contact you again, do not say a word until I've arrived. They're aware you're now represented by council and that they're not allowed to speak to you without me."

"Got it. Thanks, Julia," Vesper replied. "Appreciate everything you've done for me."

Julia smiled, nodded a goodbye to both of us, then headed to the parking lot and got in her car.

Vesper turned to me. "So, how's the investigation coming?"

I shrugged. "I'd like to tell you I know who killed Tony, but that would be a lie. I'm leaning toward Daniel, though."

"Really?"

"Sharky Boards wasn't doing as well as Tony and Daniel had been making it out to be. I'm thinking maybe Daniel blamed Tony for a few of the more questionable decisions and figured the company would be better off with just him in charge. Oh, and someone was blackmailing Tony too. You wouldn't happen to know anything about that, would you?"

"Definitely not, but I'm intrigued. Who was it?"

"We don't know. It's untraceable. What did the police have on you? Why did they arrest you?"

"The knife that was used to kill Tony. Apparently, they figured out the brand name, and they found out I own the same one. Of course I do. I bought my knife set at Target. It's the cheapest one they had, and I'm sure half the island has the same set. They came in with a search warrant. Didn't tell me what they were after, just barged into my place. I asked Jake if I could help him look for something, but he told me I should just call my lawyer. So I did. Thirty seconds later, that other cop comes out. The fat one who works with Jake, looks like a ball sack with eyes."

"Liam," I confirmed.

"Yeah, that's the one. He comes out, nods at Jake, then looks at me and tells me I'm under arrest. Then he puts me in cuffs and leads me out. That's when we saw you."

"You were smart not to talk to them without a lawyer."

"I didn't know what they were after. Pigs. They ruined my night because they didn't bother asking, just assumed they were right. We got to the police station, and Jake gave me a phone to call Julia. Then they put me in one of those interrogation rooms. Left me alone in there. I know the strategy. It's to throw you off. You're by yourself in the little gray room, and they think leaving you alone with your thoughts is going to make you more likely to confess. Well, too bad for them. I have raging, undiagnosed ADHD, and I am more than comfortable sitting alone with my thoughts all day."

I let out a small chuckle. "So they didn't get anything out of you?"

"Nope. Liam came over and brought me a glass

of water, but I know better than to give them my fingerprints and DNA for free."

"Good."

"It's like those morons think none of us have ever watched an episode of *CSI*. Anyway, Julia showed up eventually, and she's just an absolute doll. I love her. I wish she was gay. I wish I was gay too. For a lot of reasons, but for one thing, I wouldn't be in this situation if I was. Anyway, she came in and immediately took over. Damn, I wish I had the power to make people feel like that when I walk into a room. Julia told the cops we needed some time and that they weren't allowed to listen in on what we said. They immediately did as she asked, and we were alone in the room."

"What did she tell you?"

"About the knife, for one thing. At that point, I still didn't know what they found at my place that led to me getting arrested. She told me they had come with a warrant to search for a certain set of knives and specifically to see whether the knife that matched the one that killed Tony was missing."

"And it was?" I asked.

"Well, it wasn't in the knife block. But it wasn't missing."

"Where was it?"

"In my bedroom. That's where it always is. I don't need a chef's knife to cook. I'm not Gordon fucking Ramsey. The middle knife is fine."

231

"So, uh, what's the other knife doing in your bedroom?"

"Protection," Vesper replied as if I was the dumb one for asking. "You never know what kind of creep is going to come into my place in the middle of the night, and if someone wants to try something with me, they're going to have to earn it."

"Well, honestly, that's probably the least weird answer you could have given me."

"I have a secret compartment built into the headboard of my bed. That's where I keep it, along with Dildo Daggins, so they're both within easy reach."

"Dildo Daggins?"

"He's very good at finding things that are hidden in the dark," Vesper said with a wink.

"Well, I'm never going to be able to watch those movies again."

"You're such a prude. Anyway, I told Julia all of this. And she was much more understanding about Dildo Daggins."

"Please stop saying that name out loud."

"Julia told me I was going to tell the cops what I just told you, and she called them in. It was Liam and someone else. I get the impression he was Liam's boss, but I don't know for sure. Anyway, I told them where the knife was, and the boss gave Liam a look that probably made his butthole pucker worse than a chili-flavored donut. They left without a word, and Julia told me to hold tight. Twenty minutes later, I was told I was free to go, and we left. You know the rest."

I burst out laughing. "Wow. That's definitely a story."

"There were other officers still searching my place. Liam called them, and somebody found the knife exactly where I'd left it. Given as I didn't kill Tony."

"Well, for what it's worth, I never thought you did. That's why I came over here—to yell at Jake and tell him to let you go and do an investigation properly."

"I hope you got through to him. Julia certainly did. I heard her giving the other guy an earful. The words 'unlawful arrest' and 'lawsuit' came up."

"Good. So, do you need a ride home?"

"That'd be nice, but if you have other plans, I can figure something out."

"I'm pissed at Jake, I'm pissed at the gangsters in Seattle that are trying to kill me, and I'm running on adrenaline right now. I can drop you off, no problem, but I'm not sure what I'm doing next."

"Oh, honey, we're going to do something else, then. The cops are probably still at my place anyway. Have any other cases on the go?"

"One. An unknown intruder at a building near here." Rosie was careful enough about her privacy that I wasn't about to tell Vesper this was where she lived. "I need to go stake out the place a little."

"Well, why don't I join you?"

"On one condition."

"What's that?"

"Under no circumstances are we allowed to talk about dildos."

Vesper laughed. "Kids these days have no sense of humor. You got yourself a deal."

The two of us hopped into Queenie and drove to Rosie's building. I parked across the street so as to not draw suspicion to us and I walked Vesper through what had been going on. "The problem is, from here, we can't see what's going on inside. And if we're inside, we're open to more questions. And that has to be where the intruder is coming from."

"Does it, though? All these properties have exterior balconies," Vesper pointed out.

"Yeah, but some of the thefts took place on the third floor. There aren't any fire escapes or easy ways to get up there."

"If someone wants to rob you, they'll find a way. I live on the third floor, and I still keep a knife in my bedhead, just in case."

"How many times has the knife come in handy, though?"

"Only once, but that had nothing to do with a burglar," Vesper admitted.

"I don't even want to know," I muttered.

"No, you probably don't. Still, it's possible."

"It is, but the higher floors are safer than you think from the outside. I leave the windows in our place open when I'm gone all the time. But then again, I also don't leave jewelry just lying around."

"How do you know it's someone who lives in the building, anyway?"

"I don't. But they're only hitting up this building, as far as we know, and the security is pretty tight."

"Have you tested it?"

"No, but there's a key fob system at the front entrance."

"Honey, those are easy as pie to get past."

"Please don't mention pie; I should be eating the first of my free year's worth by now. Anyway, we should probably test it," I admitted.

Vesper and I got out of the car and walked to the front door. Vesper immediately began hitting the buttons for entry, and a moment later, a man's voice came over the speakerphone.

"Yes?"

"Hi, I have a pizza for John," Vesper said brightly.

"Wrong apartment," the voice on the other end snapped.

"Oh, my bad, must have pressed the wrong button. Would you mind just buzzing me in?"

A moment later, the door beeped, and I pulled it

open, raising my eyebrows at Vesper. Rosie had said it to me before: the biggest flaw in security was always, always people.

I pulled it open, and Rosie and I stepped inside.

"Okay, so we're here," I said quietly, standing in the main lobby. To the right and left were the apartments. "Now what? It's not like the person doing this is just going to show themselves."

"No, but we've proven they don't have to be a resident of this building to be the thief."

"Great. We've just expanded our suspect pool by literally thousands of people."

"Hey, it's better than not having a clue, isn't it?" Vesper had a point there. "So, who all lives here that you know of?"

"Well, there's a drug dealer who lives down that way. And one of his customers lives just upstairs. There's an empty apartment, as well, that they're trying to rent out at a price that would make your eyes water but that they'll probably get. And then also upstairs, there's a woman who makes a super weird pineapple drink that would pass exactly zero safety inspections and sells it on TikTok."

"Oh, I've seen that."

"The drink?"

Vesper nodded. "One of the kids on the beach showed it to me about two weeks ago."

"Please don't tell me they were drinking it."

Vesper laughed. "No. They were more horrified

by it. They knew it was someone on the island selling it, since she makes it a selling point to say she's on Maui but only uses pineapples from small, locally owned farms."

"Which, honestly, is a selling point. It's just that while I want my sustainable fruit grown by people making a living wage and by people who have lived off this land for centuries rather than exploiting it, I also want it to not have bits of glitter in it."

"Exactly."

The two of us walked casually down the hall in the opposite direction from where I'd gone the other day.

"You never know what you're going to find down here," I said quietly. "We might as well give it a look."

We passed by an older woman, at least in her seventies, who shuffled past us with a suspicious look.

"Hi," I greeted her politely as we walked past, flashing her a smile. She replied with a barely concealed glare.

When we had done a whole circle of the ground floor without seeing a single other person, Vesper and I took the elevator up to the second floor.

"This is a quiet building," Vesper said. "No one is doing anything. And yet there's a thief around."

"I think they're taking advantage," I replied. "It seems like a lot of the residents here are long-timers, which means a lot of them know and trust each other."

Before Vesper had a chance to agree, pain seared through my back. I let out a small yelp as I collapsed to the ground, my muscles refusing to do what they were supposed to. I knew this feeling. I knew it all too well. I'd been Tasered.

Chapter 21

I fought to stay awake. The edges of my vision got blurry, and darkness started setting in around the edges of the world, but I blinked hard and forced myself to fight through the pain.

"What the hell is wrong with you?" I heard Vesper shouting as I blinked, focusing on my breathing.

"I want an explanation, and I want it now. Thieves!"

I rolled over with a groan and looked over at my attacker. It was the seventy-something woman from downstairs. Of course it was. Braced in a wide stance, she was still pointing the Taser at me with both hands.

I picked the probes out of my clothes and threw them at the floor. "Come on, lady," I said to her. "What are you doing?"

"You're the thief," she snarled at us.

I raised my eyebrows. "The thief?"

"The one who's been going around stealing from this property. Don't think I don't recognize you. You're the young woman who was here the other day, checking out the vacant property with your supposed grandmother. I met her in the parking lot."

"What thief are you talking about? Yes, that was me. Obviously. I'm not hiding that. I came back here to show my mother around so she can have a look and help us figure out what the best place for my grandmother is," I snapped back at her, thinking quickly.

"This isn't your mother."

"Why, because I only have one leg? That's discrimination," Vesper shot at her.

"No, because I spoke with your grandmother, and she hates your mother."

"You think I don't know that? You think I don't realize that crazy bitch thinks we're all after her money, even though she has more of it than God himself? She's like that damned dragon in the Hobbit movies, sitting on her hoard, terrified that anyone who gets close is going to steal whatever they were after. I don't know. I never watched the third movie."

Vesper snorted. I was hoping Vesper wasn't going to mention Bilbo's name. After tonight, I was going to have to wipe my brain for a while before I'd be able to look at those movies without thinking about the dildo in her nightstand.

"It's the middle of the night. Where is Gareth?"

"We didn't want to be given a guided tour. We wanted to see what this place was like without him trying to sanitize everything for us," I snapped, finally feeling decent enough to get up off the floor. "He tried to hide the fact that there was a thief from us, so we thought we would have a look around and see what things were like when he wasn't here. And I'm getting an idea: paranoid old folks walking around Tasering random people."

"I thought you were a thief."

"Yeah, well, I thought you were a bitch when we walked past each other and you didn't say hello, but I didn't assault you, did I? Even though, as it turns out, only one of us was right," I replied, glaring at her.

"I'm still not convinced you aren't the thief."

"Well, I'm convinced you really are a bitch. You realize assault is a crime, right? I could call the police right now and have you arrested."

"So is theft."

"And I haven't stolen anything. Who do you think the police are going to believe? The old lady who somehow carries a Taser around, using it on people who dare to be in a hallway after seven o'clock, or the woman who's just out here trying to find a nice place for her grandmother to live out her days?"

The two of us glared at each other, and finally, the old lady put the Taser down. "Fine," she snapped. "I'm going back to my apartment. But I'm keeping my eye on you." She narrowed her eyes and carefully stepped back. "Don't follow me, either. I don't want you knowing what apartment I live in."

"Don't worry. My dream in life is that I never have to see you again," I shot back at her.

The woman took a few more steps back then continued down the hall. Eventually, she entered the stairwell next to the elevator.

I looked over at Vesper. "I can't say I was expecting to get Tasered here tonight."

"And by a senior citizen, no less."

"This is what's bugging me, though," I said as we walked back down the hall in the opposite direction that the lady had gone. "A lot of the people in this building are obviously worried. They're keeping an eye out. Not everyone, sure. But all you need is a single overly enthusiastic person with a Taser, and there's a good chance that if someone *is* coming in here stealing, they're going to get caught."

"I suppose that gives a bit more credence to your idea that the thief is someone in the building," Vesper said. "They would be able to move around the halls without drawing suspicion the way we just did."

I nodded. "Yeah. It's one of the reasons I think it's a resident. But we're not going to get anywhere here tonight, I don't think."

"No," Vesper admitted. "Why don't we hang out in the car and watch the windows? See if anyone appears who looks like they don't belong. Maybe catch the thief in the act from there."

"That's probably our best bet," I agreed. "We can't see all the windows in this place from the one side, but we can see about half of them."

We took the stairs at the end of the hall and were walking back toward the main entrance when suddenly, I paused. Walking up to the front door were two uniformed police officers.

"Shit," I hissed, grabbing Vesper and pulling her out of view. "Cops."

"That old lady probably called 9-1-1 before she even got to us," Vesper spat.

I looked around, my eyes landing on Samuel's door. "Over here."

I grabbed my lock-picking tool from my bag and did the fastest unlocking job of my life. Vesper and I launched ourselves inside, and I quickly shut the door behind us. I figured this was the safest apartment to hide in. Samuel, for very obvious reasons, wouldn't want to attract the attention of the police if he was in here, and I was sure we could easily convince him to let us leave from the balcony at the back.

But down the hall, the sound of water splattering against the tile of the shower made it obvious that wasn't going to be a problem. Then, cutting through the water, came the sound of singing.

"Is that… Taylor Swift?" Vesper whispered, looking curiously down the hall.

Sure enough, Samuel was belting out the lyrics to "Bad Blood." "I think we can all relate to that," I said.

Vesper nodded sagely in agreement.

"Now, come on," I continued. "We have to get out of here." My eyes landed on the balcony door leading outside. The ground floor–level apartments had a three-foot-tall railing that separated their balconies from the rest of the shared space on the property. We were three feet away from freedom. It wasn't as if the cops were going to have this place surrounded.

I looked over to see Vesper checking out Samuel's drug collection on the coffee table. He had obviously been hard at work since the other day; there was now more cocaine and less weed.

"Vesper," I hissed at her. "Come on. We have to go."

"I'm coming, I'm coming," she said, grabbing a couple bricks of weed and one of coke.

"You can't take that! Leave that there!"

"Why? He's a drug dealer. And how's he going to know?"

"Oh my God. There are cops trying to find us. And you don't have a purse. Do you really want to run across that lawn carrying a ton of drugs with the police chasing you?"

Vesper rolled her eyes. "You're so dramatic. You need some weed to loosen you up. It's fine. I always have a built-in storage space."

She reached down, grabbed her prosthetic leg, and clicked the button that released the strap holding it tightly to her stump. Vesper shoved the drugs into the gap and put her leg back on. "See? Problem solved. The cops never think to check your legs for drugs."

I blinked hard, trying to figure out if I was dreaming. Vesper had told me in the past that she'd gotten away with smuggling drugs in her leg. I had never been sure if she was telling the truth, but it really didn't look like this was her first time doing this.

"Okay, now that you've stolen from a drug dealer, we *really* need to go," I said, glancing nervously down the hall.

"Fine, fine," Vesper said. I opened the balcony door gingerly in case it was a squeaker—now that Vesper had helped herself to some of Samuel's stash, the last thing I wanted was for him to hear us in his apartment—but luckily, the rollers were smooth. We crept out, and I closed the door behind us.

Vesper was the first to go over the balcony railing. She moved more deftly than I expected for a woman with only one leg, but then again, she was an athlete. I struggled just a little bit more, throwing one leg over the railing and painfully sliding across before losing my balance and face-planting into the grass on the other side.

"Come on, Not Simone Biles," Vesper said.

"Oh, like you can talk, Willie Nelson," I shot back.

I struggled to my feet, and the two of us sprinted across the street, where we practically dove into Queenie. I started the car and pulled out onto the street, my heart racing.

"That isn't how I expected tonight to go," I finally said as we drove up South Kihei Road. An idea was forming in my head, though. I was pretty sure I knew who the thief was. I just had to prove it.

"I've been arrested twice in one night a few times. It kind of loses its luster after the first time, though."

"I'm personally hoping to never find out."

I pulled Queenie back into my parking spot at our apartment complex, and Vesper flashed me a grin. "That was a better night than I could have imagined, although I don't think you're any closer to solving your case. Too bad. It was fun."

I laughed. "Spoken like someone who didn't get Tasered."

"Fair enough. Thanks for the ride. Grabbing a cab would have been much less interesting."

"Good night, Vesper."

She climbed out of the car and tapped the frame a couple of times before heading inside. I was about to climb out myself and head in, but my phone binged just then. It was Dot.

Brady is on the move, and he's driving in the direction of your place.

I got out of the car and rushed inside after Vesper.

Chapter 22

A s soon as I entered the apartment, I made sure the blinds were shut tight. I didn't want Brady Ludlam to have the opportunity to see me here, in my home. Knowing I was being followed was unnerving. I didn't like it. I didn't like not knowing what they were going to do next or how they were going to act. Maybe there was something to Vesper's secret bedroom knife for protection. Or Dot's twenty-seven hidden guns.

I paced around the living room, and Coco lifted her head from the spot on the couch where she'd been curled up in a ball, napping. She must have sensed something was wrong.

"Sorry, girl," I said, offering her a tight smile. I went to the kitchen and grabbed a Bud Light from the fridge. If there was ever a night for beer, it was this one.

I popped the cap off and took a swig right as my phone began to ring. It was Dot.

"What have you got?" I asked when I answered, immediately putting the phone on speaker and leaving it on the counter while I drank.

"He's just pulled into your apartment block," Dot said. "We're driving past so as to not draw attention to ourselves, and we'll keep an eye on him. Rosie just got out of the car. Stay where you are. She's armed. If he tries anything, she'll take care of it."

A wave of nausea rose into my throat. Great. This was really happening. Well, armed or not, if Brady tried busting his way into my apartment, he was going to get more than he bargained for. I immediately grabbed Coco and locked her in the bedroom. She looked a bit confused, but Coco loved being on the bed, and I knew she'd be asleep in about fifteen seconds flat. If Brady came in here, there was no way he was going to hurt Coco.

Next, I went to the kitchen and grabbed the biggest knife from the chopping block. I placed it on top of one of the drawers on the kitchen island, out of sight, so I could easily grab it if I needed to. The element of surprise was going to be my biggest draw here.

"Okay," I said to Dot. "If he comes after me, I'm ready."

Ready to take him on, I grabbed my phone and

hid in the closet with a baseball bat. There was an eighth-of-an-inch gap between the two closet doors when they were closed, just wide enough that I could peek through and see what was happening. If he broke in, I'd wait for him to pass me and take him out with the bat. If something went wrong, I knew exactly where the knife was hidden.

"Stand down. False alarm," Dot said. "He's driving back out. I see him now."

"You're sure?"

"Yup. I have eyes on him. I'll follow."

A wave of relief washed over me. I wasn't going to be attacked tonight.

"It looked like he's heading back to his apartment, but I'll make sure," Dot continued.

Just then, there was a knock at my door, and I jumped about three feet in the air.

"It's just me," Rosie's voice said.

I exited the closet, double-checked through the peep hole just to be sure, then opened the door to let her in.

"Dot, I have Rosie here," I said into the phone.

"Hi, Dot. I'm glad you thought to follow him."

"What did he do?" Dot asked.

"Went straight over to Charlie's Jeep. He left a note on the dashboard then walked up to the front door. He tried it, had a look at the security, then got back into his car and drove off."

"What did the note say?" I asked.

251

Rosie reached into her pocket and pulled out a folded piece of paper. She handed it to me, and I pulled it open.

I read the note out loud. "We're coming for you, bitch. You killed Stevie, now you have to die."

"That's rather uninspired as far as death threats go," Dot said.

"He obviously doesn't spend nearly enough time on the internet," I agreed. I began rolling my weight back and forth from my toes to my heels as I pulsated with anger. I looked at the faces before me. A few minutes ago, I'd been scared. And honestly, who could have blamed me? The same people who had left a finger at my doorstep as a message had now left me an even more explicit threat. They wanted to kill me.

But I had people on my side. I had Dot and Rosie, who had been shadowing the guy for a day just to make sure I was safe. I had Zoe, who I knew would do anything for me and was the best friend anyone could ask for. And I had Jake, who would protect me however he had to.

The Ham brothers had no idea what they'd gotten into. I wasn't a lonely, almost-thirty-year-old living by myself with no idea what I was doing in life anymore. I had friends. Friends I could rely on. Friends they wouldn't see coming and who would help me completely destroy them.

I tore the letter in half, and I could feel Dot

grinning on the other end of the line. "Brady can tell me whatever he wants. He's not getting back to Seattle. I have an idea."

"Does it involve murder?" Rosie asked. "Because if so, I can ensure the body is never found."

I shook my head. "No. But I might need your help. I'll let you know tomorrow. I'll think about this overnight, come up with a plan."

"Whatever you need, we're here," Dot said.

"Absolutely," Rosie agreed.

My face flushed with warmth from the love my friends were sending me right now. They would follow me anywhere if it meant saving my life, and there was nothing in the world that felt better than knowing I had my people by my side.

"Thanks. Listen, Rosie, I'm going to drop you off at your place, okay? I have an idea who the thief is, and I want to be sure."

"Wow, you've figured it out?"

"Vesper came with me earlier, and we had a look. It was something she said. I'm not a hundred percent sure, but I have an idea, and I want to test it out."

"Speaking of Vesper, how did things go at the police station?" I had sent Dot and Rosie a quick update text while I was on the way.

"Fine. The police searched her apartment, though. They were trying to see if the murder weapon was missing from her knife set. Which it was, but it wasn't where they thought."

"They didn't check the compartment in her headboard where she keeps Dildo Daggins," Dot said knowingly.

"How on *earth* do you know about that?"

"Because some of us aren't pearl clutchers who faint the instant something remotely sexual is mentioned."

"I do not do that."

"You once threatened to set yourself on fire in front of me because I tried to give you some advice on something Jake might like that I read in a magazine."

"Your advice involved anal beads. I want to set myself on fire *now*."

"No one is setting themselves on fire," Rosie said.

"Dot has to stop talking about Vesper's dildo, then. You know what? *Everyone* needs to stop talking about it."

"Then let's get back to the thief," Rosie said. "Is there anything I can do to help?"

I let out a small giggle. "One of your neighbors thinks I'm the thief, so uh, it might not be the best idea to be seen with me right now."

"Understood."

"Right," Dot said. "I'll head home then, and I'll keep an eye on the two of you in the morning. I'm going to throw a tracker on Brady's car just to be safe. If he moves, day or night, I'll get an alert."

We said goodbye to Dot and hung up the phone.

"Who do you think the thief is?" Rosie asked.

"This is going to sound ridiculous when I first say it, but stick with me: I think it's a cat."

Rosie tilted her head slightly to the side, nodding slowly. "A cat. You know, that does make sense, actually. I can't believe we didn't think of it sooner. Especially because one of the items taken was a fish. We all know food is getting more and more expensive these days, but come on. Stealing jewelry and a fish?"

"When Dot was outside, speaking with the other residents, one of them mentioned that the family that had formerly lived in the empty apartment we were looking at had had a cat and that they believed it was left behind when they moved out."

"Someone mentioned that in the Facebook group made for people who live in the complex. I did see the post, although I've never seen the cat. I never considered it could be the one behind everything. But it makes sense. Also, it would explain how someone got up onto the third floor. It wasn't a person."

"How did you figure it out?"

"When I was talking through the case with Vesper, I mentioned that I often leave the windows open because we live on the third floor, and there's no way anybody who wasn't trained in the circus could get inside that way."

Rosie pursed her lips in a way that told me she disagreed with that statement but wasn't going to say anything.

"Okay, fine. Maybe not the circus. Maybe just the KGB. But suffice to say, the number of people who would be willing and able to get up to my third-floor window to rob me can probably be counted on one hand."

"I agree with you there."

"And so we've been assuming it's someone going in through the front doors. What if it isn't? What if it's someone going in through open windows? Or some*thing*. In this case, a cat attracted by fish and shiny things."

Rosie barked out a laugh. "Wouldn't that be something, if this entire time, the thief in our complex was a poor abandoned cat? I can't believe it."

"Well, I don't know for sure just yet. Let me grab Coco's carrier just in case, and then we'll head to your place. If it is the cat, I want to find his stash, and then we need to catch him and find him a good home."

"It's awful that some people see pets as just another belonging, something to be discarded when they're finished with it, rather than a lifelong commitment. And I understand that emergency situations happen, but there are ways to deal with the rehoming of a pet that don't involve simply throwing it outside and leaving it to fend for itself." Rosie shook her head sadly. "The poor thing."

"I agree. Either way, if it's out there, we'll find it."

I grabbed Coco's little carrier just in case we needed it, and Rosie and I went downstairs and hopped into the car. On the way, we stopped at the grocery store and grabbed a few supplies, and before I knew it, we were parked at Rosie's complex.

"You should go inside," I suggested. "One of your neighbors called the cops on me tonight, so you probably don't want to be seen with me."

Rosie turned and gave me an appraising look. "You know what? If it really is a cat, this can wait until tomorrow. You're exhausted."

"Is it that obvious?"

"To someone who knows you well, yes. You don't have to do everything all at once. We've got everything we need here. Let's just do this tomorrow after you get a good night's sleep."

Tension in my shoulders released then, melting away like butter in a hot pan, and I leaned back against the driver's seat. "Okay, that honestly does sound like a good idea. But tomorrow, I'll be here, and we'll see if I'm right."

"Great," Rosie said. "Good night, Charlie."

"Night, Rosie."

As I pulled out of the parking lot, I stifled a yawn. I really was exhausted, both mentally and physically. I didn't feel like I was any closer to finding out who had killed Tony, but hopefully tomorrow would bring some answers. I had a pretty good idea who the thief at Rosie's place was.

I got home, thinking I could mull over the evidence I had in Tony's case while I got to sleep, but the last couple of days caught up with me, and I was out for good pretty much immediately.

The last thing I remembered was Coco curling up into a ball in the crook of my knees.

Chapter 23

I woke up around nine the next morning. I stretched and then threw on some clothes and shuffled into the kitchen, wiping the sleep from my eyes. Zoe was fussing around, getting ready to go to work.

"How are things going with the gangsters?" she asked when she saw me, a worried expression on her face.

"It's going to be taken care of today," I said firmly. "I'm not letting them get to me. Am I scared? Yeah, if I'm honest, I am. But I'm also angry. They don't get to take my life away just because of something that wasn't my fault. It's not like I went out there looking for Stevie. I was just trying to sell enough jewelry to not get fired. They don't get to come in here and ruin my life."

A twinkle appeared in Zoe's eye as the corner of

her mouth curled upward into a smile. "There's the Charlie I know. Just try not to blow anything up on the way, will you? Or get Tasered."

"Don't worry. That already happened yesterday. The Taser thing, not the blowing-things-up thing."

"I literally can't even tell if you're joking."

"I'm not."

"When you die, you should donate your body to science, because I don't think there's a single person out there who has ever found themselves on the receiving end of that much electricity. Seriously, I want you to make an appointment with your doctor to get an EKG to look at your heart, just in case."

"I'm fine. My heart always sounds okay."

"That's what people who die of heart attacks say, until one day, it doesn't."

"Okay. If it'll make you feel better, I'll do it."

"Thank you."

"Although if those gangsters have anything to do with it, they're probably going to try and make sure I die of lead poisoning."

"You won't," Zoe said firmly.

"No. And you also don't need to worry. Dorothy is tracking the guy's car. She's keeping an eye on him, and if anything happens, she'll be there. And so will Rosie. They're both on alert right now."

"You know, there's nobody in the world I'd rather have hunting them down than those two ladies."

"Me either. Plus they have the added advantage that no one ever suspects them."

"Exactly. It's funny. Everyone always trusts women not to commit crimes against them but doesn't believe women when they tell them things they don't like. We just get labeled crazy. Last night, I had a patient who demanded to be seen by a male doctor because women are 'too emotional' to be doctors."

I raised an eyebrow skyward. "I bet that went over well."

"I told him all the doctors on the floor for the night were women, so he had the option of seeing me, or he could just hang out in the waiting room for another twelve hours for shift change."

"What did he go with?"

"Daring to let a female doctor deal with his issue. Which was just a small infection. I could have given him the antibiotic injection and prescription for an oral dose of amoxicillin in my sleep. Still, he said he was going to google everything before he took it, just in case. I told him to make sure a man wrote the article and not a woman, and he agreed. Didn't catch the sarcasm in my voice at all."

"Of course not. How lovely to have gone to school for a billion years only to be told that you're too emotional to do your job."

Zoe grinned. "Still more than worth it, though."

"I bet. You probably see fewer butts than I do.

Actually, no. I think we probably see a similar number of butts."

"That's probably not the measuring stick I would use to compare our careers," Zoe said with a giggle. "But it works."

"Luckily, this case has had zero requirements to get proof of cheating husbands. It seems like for the first time in his life, Tony was actually in a monoga-mous relationship. Everyone is surprised about it."

"Have you spoken to Lily?"

"Yeah. She did understand that when she gave him that kidney, it wasn't a promise that he would be with her forever too."

"Good. It's always a risk in situations like that. I know transplants from living donors sometimes happen, but they usually come from a family member or a complete stranger. It's rare for some-one's girlfriend that they met just a few weeks earlier to happen to be a perfect match. And the nature of the relationship means the power dynamic shifts with the donation. So if Lily is aware of that, and she never expected him to be tied to her forever, then that's good."

"Yeah. She was obviously broken up about it. And there's no sign at all that Tony was cheating on her. I think he really was making an effort to be with her forever. I suppose they were, in the end.

"I'm going to see Daniel again today. He lied to me about the state of the business."

"You think he could have done this?"

"Yes. He was in the water, he tried to steer me toward the exes, and he hid the fact that the business was in trouble from me. Right now, I consider him a prime suspect."

"Okay. Well, I have to get going. Good luck finding your killer. Try not to get Tasered again. Or in too much other trouble. Right now, the list is too long to go through." Zoe reached over and gave me a hug. "I love you, Charlie. Take care of yourself, okay?"

"I love you too. Thanks."

Zoe grabbed her bag and left, and I pulled out my notepad to have a look at the notes I'd taken before driving up to Paia. I needed to be sure of everything before I spoke to Daniel again.

I LET COCO OUT TO DO HER BUSINESS AND STARTED about my day soon afterward, and at around ten-thirty, I found my way to the Sharky Boards factory headquarters. I grabbed a coffee to give me a little pick-me-up on the way. The factory was located a bit more inland than Tony's home, along Baldwin Avenue, a couple of miles from the beach, not too far from the local church and elementary school. These sleepy Hawaiian back roads were my favorite spots on the island. Away from the hustle and bustle of the tourist centers, this was where life still moved at a slower pace, where it always looked like nature was pushing in, trying to reclaim the earth humans had built over but that weren't used enough, like the sidewalk that looked more like stepping stones these days.

I pulled into the dusty, unpaved parking lot and had a look around. This was definitely not a luxury boutique. The couple patches of grass around the building were yellow and looked as if they'd snap like a twig if a stiff breeze hit them. The factory and sales building itself was a single-story building with a corrugated iron roof that had seen better days. On the left-hand side was a small dock that led to a loading zone, and a sign above the front door announced the company's name.

Next to the door, an enormous wood version of the company logo took center stage, and I had to admit, it did look pretty good. Clearly, the sign was where all of the exterior decorating budget had gone. But hey, the boards were good quality from everything I'd heard, and that was obviously the most important part.

When I walked inside, however, things were different. The interior was bright and spacious. This was a sales floor and administration office. Directly in front of me was an enormous desk, behind which sat a woman in her twenties. To the left were surfboards, all sorts of different shapes, sizes, and colors, ready to be purchased by whoever needed that particular model. On the right were a large variety of surf accessories on shelves: rash guards, dry bags, wetsuits, neoprene booties, changing towels, and a million other things I didn't recognize.

Against the far wall, behind the front counter, two doors on either side had "Staff only" written across them.

"Hi there," the woman behind the counter greeted me in a voice that was far too chirpy for a Monday morning. "How can I help you today?"

"Hi. I'm hoping to speak to Daniel today. He suggested I stop by. I'm Charlie Gibson. I'm investigating Tony's death.

The smile immediately faded from the woman's face and was replaced with a sad shake of her head. "I still can't believe it. It doesn't feel real. I still half expected him to walk through that door this morning, like he always did, with a tip of his hat and a "Hi, Carly!" like he did every single day. You're the private investigator?"

I nodded. "That's me."

"Daniel said when he arrived that you might come in. I can take you right to him."

I paused. "Before you do that, do you mind if I ask you a few questions? Just about Tony, what he was like, and how everything was going at work. Just getting different perspectives, you know?"

Carly paused, a flicker of surprise passing over

her features for a second, then sat back in her chair with a nod. "Oh, sure. Yeah. I don't think I have anything that can help you find the killer, but if I can help, I will."

"How was Tony at work? How did he act? Was there anything strange going on?"

Carly bit her lip as she considered my question. "Things were mostly normal. Tony was happy, you know? He had gotten that transplant he needed ago, and you have no idea how much it changed him. Made him into a new man entirely. Before, when he was going to Kahului for dialysis regularly, he looked like he was on the brink of death sometimes. I genuinely didn't think he was going to make it until they found him a donor from the transplant list. But he got lucky; Lily was a match, and he got his new kidney. After that, he was just... well, he was normal. Normal, but with the knowledge that he had cheated death and was going to take advantage of every day. I can't believe he got so little time."

"But in the past few weeks, you didn't see any changes?"

"No," Carly said. "Not really. Although there was something in the mail he didn't like."

"Oh?"

"Every week or so, he began getting a regular letter, starting about six weeks before he died. It was typed, just a plain envelope. Anyway, the second time it came in, he stared at it for a while. I asked him if everything was okay, and he said it was fine, but I still wondered. Then another came in a week later, and as soon as he saw, it he scrunched it up but then took it with him to his office. I didn't dare ask about it."

"Did you ever snoop to find out what was in it? Seriously, if you did, I don't care. I won't tell anyone. I just need to know on the chance that it will help us find who killed him."

Carly's shoulders slumped. "Sorry. I wish I had now. I wanted to, don't get me wrong. But I also got the feeling if I snooped, Tony would be pissed. And my job is more important than knowing what those letters were. Anyway, after that, he just took the mail and went into his office to read it. I haven't got a clue what was in those envelopes."

I nodded slowly. I had a sneaking suspicion that that was where the blackmail had been coming from. He must have been taking those letters home with him, where Jake and the cops found them.

"Did Tony get along with everyone here at the company?" I asked.

"Yeah. Sure. I mean, he was the boss. There were times when he had to be a bit strict or to tell people off for doing something incorrectly, but that was all just normal work stuff. I don't think he was unfair to anyone."

"He worked mainly on the factory floor, right?"

"Yes, but we all share a single break room. We talk. If there was something actually going on, then I would know about it."

I nodded. Daniel was the one who had told me to come and speak with one of the employees, Andrew. Was that because he was trying to steer suspicion away from himself? I wondered.

"Okay, thanks. What about Daniel? Were he and Tony getting along, do you know?"

Carly's gaze shifted to the left. "Yeah, fine."

"Are you sure? Listen, I just want to find the person who killed Tony." I lowered my voice. "If that happens to be Daniel, do you really want to keep working only a few feet away from someone who slammed a chef's knife into the back of another human being?"

I purposely looked slowly at the door just a couple feet away from Carly. Her mouth gaped slightly, her eyes widening as she considered the gravity of my statement. "You're right. But look, if he didn't do this, you're not going to go after him, are you? This is a good job. I like it here. Daniel is a nice boss and way better than a few others I've had."

"I'm only out to find the truth, whatever that may be."

Carly nodded. "In that case, you should know, I think there were some arguments happening between them. But you didn't hear that from me."

"I will be discreet when I talk to Daniel. Don't worry. Could you hear the arguments?"

"Only once. I stayed late. I'm doing part-time coursework, and I wanted to use my work computer to upload some files because the internet connection here is faster than the one I have at home. But I don't think either one of them knew I was still at work, because I went to the break room while my files were uploading. I'm at film school at UH," Carly explained. "So the files I had to upload were big, and I knew it would take a while, so I went to grab a snack before I went home. The break room is across from Daniel's office. While I was eating, I heard them arguing."

"What about?"

"About the company. Money, I think. Daniel said they were hemorrhaging it. Tony said they were investing in the future and that getting the sales now would mean they were growing quickly."

"What did Daniel reply?"

"He said that Tony wasn't finding enough people to fill the orders they had and that they were falling behind. He was worried about the company's reputation. He was getting phone calls from irate customers wondering where their boards were. He said the company was unbalanced. They argued for a while. Tony said he would find more workers for the factory but that ultimately, the company would grow. Daniel said the numbers had them face-planting."

I nodded, and Carly looked at me curiously.

"Did you know about this? Is it true? Is the company really in trouble?"

"It's not my place to say," I replied. "But let's just say I agree with Daniel."

"So this place is going under," Carly said and sighed.

"Not necessarily. I mean, if Daniel isn't the killer, he seems like a smart guy."

"Oh, he is. He's a good manager."

"Do you think he can turn things around by himself?"

"I hope so. But Tony really was an expert at making boards. He knew every single inch of every single surfboard. And he was great at teaching the guys in the shop how to make them. I've been surfing my whole life, and I love Sharky Boards. It's why I applied for a job here. But Tony taught the guys well. I think Daniel will be able to keep every-thing going."

"Cool. Okay, thanks. Listen, if you think of anything else that might help, please feel free to give me a call or text. Anytime."

I slid a business card across the counter, and Carly picked it up, tapped it against the edge of the table a couple of times, then slid it into the pocket of her pants. "Will do. Now, come on. I'll take you in to see Daniel." Carly got up from her chair.

"Oh, just one more thing I have to ask," I said as she stood. I had wanted to keep this question until the end and get her a little off-balance before I asked it. "Did Tony ever hit on you? Try and get you to date him?"

My plan to catch Carly off guard failed completely as she shot me a wry smile. "Nope. But he knew it would have been pointless if he tried. I'm a lesbian."

"Ah," I said. "Good to know."

"He's devoted to Lily, anyway. I've met her a few times, and she was always very nice. I can't imagine what she's going through right now."

Without waiting for a response, Carly led me to the door on the right. We passed through and into a narrow hallway. There were five or six offices, and at the end of the hall was Daniel's.

"Here you go," she said. "Good luck. I hope you find the person who killed Tony."

"Thanks." I offered Carly a smile and then stepped inside, knowing I was about to interview someone who had already lied to me and had had every opportunity to murder Tony. Was I about to talk to a killer?

Chapter 24

Daniel's office was plain but neat. It comprised white walls, wooden furniture, a plant in the corner, and a couple of surfing-related prints on the walls to add a small splash of color.

He was tapping away at the computer when I entered, his focus on the screen of the new iMac in front of him, but as soon as he saw me, he stopped in midstroke. He stood up and reached across the desk to shake my hand.

"Charlie. I'm glad you came today. Please, have a seat." He motioned to the chair in front of the desk, plain but comfortably upholstered. "How is your investigation going?"

I pulled my shoulders back slightly, going for a firm but professional feel. "It's coming along well. I've learned quite a bit about Tony's life, but I've got some questions that I'm hoping you can help clear up for me."

"Go for it," Daniel said, casually spinning a pen between his index and middle fingers as he leaned back in his chair.

"Is it true that the company was in trouble and that you're bordering on going under?"

Daniel's relaxed demeanor immediately changed. He dropped his foot back to the ground and leaned forward over the desk, steepling his fingers. "Where did you hear that?"

"I have my sources. Tony is dead, and I had to look into everything. Is it true? Because you told me the other day on the beach that the company was doing great."

Daniel sighed, staring down at the tips of his fingers for a moment. Was he trying to collect his thoughts and tell me the truth this time, or was he figuring out how to best do damage control to stop me from finding out he was the killer?

"Okay, fine," he finally said. "The business was going through a bit of a rough patch. About eighteen months ago, Tony decided that we could grow the business really quickly. We were gaining a good reputation in the industry, and Tony thought if we brought on some more sales reps, we could really make a difference. Have them reach out to companies in California, Portugal, and Australia. You know, big markets in our space. Well, I agreed with him. But while we hired the salespeople, Tony didn't bring anyone else on to increase production. Our costs went up, but we couldn't fill orders any faster, so ultimately, we brought in virtually the same amount of money as before."

That lined up exactly with what Dot and Rosie had concluded while looking through the financial documents and what Carly had overheard.

"So the company was in trouble."

"Yes. I kept pressing Tony. I told him this had to get sorted out. And then he had the surgery, and I mean, I'm not a monster. I wasn't about to start hounding the guy immediately after he had a whole organ replaced. I left it for a few months while he recovered, but we'd been arguing about it for the past week. Tony kept telling me he was on it; he was going to find the workers for the plant. But I was out of patience. I needed him to get onto that, because otherwise, we were either going to have to fire all the new people we'd hired, or the company was going to fail. Simple as that. By my calculations, we had three months to get more people hired and producing before we passed the point of no return."

"What's going to happen now?"

Daniel expelled air up into his bangs. "Well, to be honest, I'm not sure. Obviously, this is going to be a change, with Tony gone. He was the shop manager and our lead designer, and I'm going to have to figure out who he relied on the most and who has the most potential to step into his shoes and take over. Probably one of the people who have been here the longest. I'm going to have to make that call quickly, but right now, we're in damage-control mode, as you can imagine. I need to stop the financial bleeding, but I also have to make sure that we can actually operate without Tony. How did you find out about the financial problems we were having?"

I flashed Daniel an enigmatic smile. "It's my job to find out about these things."

Daniel sat back in his chair again, though he was visibly less relaxed than at the beginning of the conversation. "I don't want to make it sound like Tony's death wasn't hard for me, because obviously, he's just been murdered. But this company, it's more than just me. We have so many employees who depend on us for a paycheck. I can't let that fail, but it's going to be tough."

"What were you going to do if Tony hadn't died?"

"What do you mean?"

"If none of the events on the beach the other day had happened and Tony was still alive, how would you be handling the financial situation? What makes you think Tony was going to change? Or did you think maybe it would be easier to get Tony out of the way permanently?"

"Are you asking if I killed him?"

I shrugged. "You have lied to me more than anybody else so far. You told me everything was fine between the two of you."

"It was. This was a business dispute. Nothing more. And do you really think I would kill my best friend over some finance issues?"

"You tell me. As you said, the whole company depended on this."

Daniel shook his head. "No. You're wrong. I never would have killed Tony, not only because he was like a brother to me but because even if I had, I'd still be in this same situation. I wouldn't have the person who leads the floor and knows exactly how to run the team that builds the boards. I'm only half the company. And I'm not arrogant enough to believe I could immediately take over for Tony. So no, I wouldn't have killed him, simply because doing so would have put the company in just as much jeopardy as him doing nothing. I'm not sure we're going to make it through this."

I nodded slowly. I believed Daniel. Everything I had seen so far told me that he was an intelligent man. He would have realized that killing Tony ultimately wouldn't have solved his problem. It just would have changed it slightly.

"Okay, I believe you," I said. Partly because it was true but partly because people had a tendency to open up a bit more when they knew they weren't suspects in a murder anymore.

"If you thought I was the killer, though, that means you don't know who really did it yet, do you? What about the police? I heard they arrested Vesper."

"And then let her go. It was a misunderstanding."

Daniel ran a hand up and down his face. "I just can't believe it. I can't believe the odds are good that I know a murderer. Someone who killed Tony. I know practically everyone who was on the water that morning."

"What about your employee, Andrew?" I asked. "The man you saw Tony talking to?"

Daniel shook his head. "No, I spoke to him. It turns out he was on Oahu last weekend, taking care of some family business. It couldn't have been him. So I asked him what he and Tony were talking about. He said he had some ideas for new board shapes he wanted to run past him. Tony had agreed to meet him outside of work. That was all it was. There was no argument."

"Okay. Did Tony ever mention to you that he was being blackmailed?"

Daniel's forehead creased. "Blackmail?"

"Yes."

"No, he never did. Are you serious? Who was it? Over what?"

"I don't know. I was hoping you could help."

"I would if I could. He never mentioned anything to me, though. Have you spoken to Lily?"

I nodded. "She didn't know, either. I suppose he didn't tell anybody."

"What would it have been over, though? That's the question."

"It is. Okay. Thanks, Daniel. If I think of anything else, I'll be in touch."

"Please feel free to speak to anyone on the floor that you need to. I want the killer found."

"I will. Thanks."

I went back to Carly at the front counter. "You wouldn't happen to know if Tony was cheating on Lily, would you?"

Carly shrugged. "I never saw any signs of it. But we all knew Tony's reputation with women."

"You don't think he was a changed man?"

"I don't think leopards change their spots, even when they get a new kidney. It's a new kidney, not all-new DNA."

"Okay, thanks."

An idea was starting to form in my head. And I wanted to see it through.

From the parking lot, I texted Jake.

Do you have time to talk?

His reply came through a moment later. *Not right now. I'm investigating a murder.*

So am I. And I think I might know who did it.

Do you have actual evidence?

Not yet.

Then come back to me when you do. I can't arrest someone based on vibes.

Wow. Someone stepped on Lego on his way out of bed this morning.

Look, can we talk later? I'm getting reamed out about the Vesper thing. And can you drop that camera you were telling me about off at some point?

Jake was obviously upset. Probably because we'd found the camera, and he hadn't.

Sure. I just have to make one more stop first. I'm in Kahului. I'll stop by your station in about an hour.

I didn't get a reply, and I was tempted to send Jake a flipping-off emoji, but instead, I did the mature thing for once and just stuck my phone in my pocket. I drove to the hospital, drumming my fingers along the steering wheel. Jake and I had never officially worked the same case before since we'd started dating. This was our first time, and it was not going as smoothly as I'd hoped.

Well, he was just going to have to get over it. We'd found that camera and he hadn't, and now he was upset. That was why he'd blown up on me yesterday. And that was too bad. In the interest of justice, he was going to have to put up with it.

Besides, I had a sneaking suspicion I was pretty close to solving this one.

I drove to the hospital, parked Queenie, and followed the signs through the labyrinthine halls until I reached the hemodialysis unit. Thanks to spending enough time around Zoe, I knew "hemo" meant blood. A woman at the counter smiled at me when I arrived. Her blond hair was tied back, and she was dressed in scrubs. I wasn't sure if she was an administrative member of staff or a nurse. She looked professional and ready and able to jump into any situation in a second.

"Hello. How can I help you?"

"Hi. My name is Charlie Gibson. I'm a private investigator, and I'm looking into the death of Tony Murray, who I understand was a patient here a few months back."

My eyes took in the scene. The woman had a number of files in a stack next to her, and she had been tapping away at the computer. Behind her were cabinets full of paperwork, I assumed.

"I'm afraid I can't give you any information on a patient for confidentiality reasons."

I smiled. "That's fine. I totally understand and wouldn't want you to tell me anything you're not allowed to share. I understand that Tony met his current girlfriend, Lily, while he was here for treatment."

The woman smiled thinly. "Yes, I believe that's right."

"Did Tony ever ask you about her?"

"I'm not going to tell you that."

"It might help me find out who killed him."

"I'm still not going to tell you. The privacy of our patients here is of the utmost importance."

Suddenly, someone called for the woman.

"Excuse me. I'll be right back."

She left, the slowly spinning chair the only sign that she had recently been here. I pursed my lips as I looked down at the pile of papers on the counter. They were barely an arm's length away.

This wasn't evidence. But I was even more convinced that I was on the right track.

Chapter 25

I stopped by Dot's apartment to pick up the camera so I could drop it off at the police station.

"I've wiped this free of all our fingerprints," Dot said as she handed it to me in a Ziploc bag. "But there's no way the police are going to get anything off this. I certainly haven't."

"Yeah, but I'm not about to reveal your superhero identity, Superhacker," I said with a wink.

"I appreciate that. Not that anyone is likely to believe you anyway if you tell them."

"That's what this whole case boils down to, I think," I said slowly. "Who to believe. And who believes whom."

"So you've figured it out?"

"I'm not one hundred percent sure yet. But I hope so."

Dot nodded. "If you need anything, you know where to find me. Brady hasn't taken his car out yet today. But he has booked a ticket home. He leaves tonight."

I inhaled sharply. I was going to have to do something now. It was time. I wasn't going to let Brady just go home and let the Ham brothers think they'd scared me senseless. It was time to go on the attack.

"Okay. Thanks."

"Do you need a hand with anything?"

"Not right now. I'm going to take care of it. But I'll let you know if things change."

"Got it."

I left Dot's place and headed back to my building, but instead of entering my apartment, I knocked on Vesper's door.

"You're a happier sight than the cops," she said. She motioned for me to enter after she opened the door. I stepped inside.

"Well, you might not agree when I'm done here. I need that coke you stole off Samuel last night."

"Is it important?"

"Very."

"Well, in that case, consider it yours. I was always more into pot anyway," Vesper said. She walked past me to the kitchen, opened one of the cupboards, then tossed me the cube she'd taken from Rosie's neighbor. "All yours."

"Thanks. I really appreciate it."

"Whatever you're doing with it, be safe."

"Oh, don't worry, I will."

I thanked Vesper again then detoured into my apartment for a second, scribbled out a quick note, then went back to the car. I immediately drove to the address where Brady was staying. I found his car, dropped off my little present, hiding it under the front seat, then texted Dot.

Let me know if Brady gets into that car, will you?

You got it.

Then I drove to the police station, stopping for another iced coffee on the way. Jake was at his desk, on the phone. Luckily, Liam was nowhere to be seen, so I sat down in his chair. It was warm. Ew. Liam butt. I forced that thought out of my head as Jake held up a finger, motioning for me to wait a minute. When he hung up the phone, he turned to me.

"What have you got?"

"The camera from Tony's home. Signed, sealed, and delivered. But I'm telling you now, you're not going to find anything on it. It's a dead end."

"I'm going to let our tech department figure that out for themselves if you don't mind," Jake said, taking it from me. "Thanks for dropping this off."

"Look, I know you're not thrilled about this case, and I don't blame you. But I need your help. About the Seattle thing."

"What do you need? It has to be legal, Charlie."

"This one hundred percent is. When I text you, I need you to find a certain Mustang. It's a rental. Here's the license plate," I said, sliding a small piece of paper across the table. "I need you to pull the driver over and come up with a reason to search his car."

Jake raised an eyebrow. "We aren't allowed to just make those things up, you know."

"And yet your fellow cops seem to have no problem doing it to innocent people regularly. Believe me, I need you to do this."

"This is important to stop the gangsters?"

"I don't think it'll stop them. But it will let them know I'm not someone to be trifled with, that I'm not afraid of them, and that they're going to have to do better than leave a threat on my windshield if they want to intimidate me."

"Shit, Charlie. What have you gotten yourself into?"

"This isn't my fault."

"I know that. But it's still dangerous. What are you doing?"

"I need you to trust me," I said, meeting his eyes squarely. "Can you do that?"

Jake took a deep breath. "I don't really have a choice here, do I?"

"Believe me. I would tell you, but it's better if it's

a fun surprise for you too. But you do need to know this guy is dangerous."

"Of course I know that," Jake said. "Fine. I'm in. Text me when you need me."

I paused. I wanted to bring up the other investigation, but it was a touchy subject with Jake, obviously. He wasn't taking it well that I was two steps ahead of him on it.

"Who are you thinking killed Tony?" Jake asked, his voice calm and level.

"I don't want to say yet."

"Because you have no evidence."

"Yeah. I'm looking into it, though."

"Look, why don't you tell me, and I'll see what legal means we can come up with to solve this?" Jake suggested.

"No. Not yet. I want to know for sure. And I don't want to scare them off."

Jake gave me a hard look. "Are you serious?"

"Yes."

"This is dangerous, Charlie."

Before I had a chance to respond, my phone binged. I pulled it out and saw a text from Dot.

He's on the move.

I jumped to my feet. "Brady is moving. We have to go."

Jake got up and grabbed his keys from the table. "Sometimes, I wonder how you talk me into these things."

Another text came through. *He's going up South Kihei Road. Given the timing, he's probably headed to Kahului.*

"He's going to the airport," I relayed to Jake.

"How do you know this?"

"Dot's following him. I'll text you any updates."

The two of us left the station, and I hopped into Queenie while Jake took a police cruiser and pulled out of the lot. We took the highway north, and when we were stopped at a set of lights, I got a text.

Are you seriously following me?

I want to see how this goes.

You said this was a dangerous gangster who left you a threat.

Yeah. That doesn't mean I don't want to see this go down.

You are insane. Absolutely insane.

I trust that you'll take care of him.

The light went green before Jake had a chance to respond, and we continued. Dot sent me the occasional update on Brady's location, which I passed on to Jake. When we were just entering Kahului, I finally spotted the car up ahead.

I tightened my grip on the steering wheel as soon as I saw it. This was it. Jake, ahead of me, pulled in behind the Mustang, and about fifteen seconds later, he turned his lights on. Brady turned on his blinkers to show he was going to pull over and turned into the parking lot of one of the nearby malls. I drove past, then turned into the next entrance.

Parking about two hundred feet away, I pulled my binoculars from the glove compartment. One thing I'd learned as a private investigator: it was always a good idea to have a pair on hand.

I adjusted the dials as I focused on the scene unfolding in front of me. Brady had his two hands out the window, a small card that was obviously his driver's license in one of them. Jake walked slowly up to him, and the two of them began to talk. I couldn't hear what was said, but Jake took the driver's license and had a look then peered into the car.

Next, with a hand on his holster, he took a step back. My heart rose into my throat. I had asked a lot from Jake here. He knew this was a dangerous gang member. Probably someone who had killed before. Someone didn't get to climb the ladder of the Ham organization without putting a few bodies in the ground first. But Jake knew what he was doing.

Brady carefully stepped out of the Mustang and took a few steps away while Jake searched the car. As soon as he reached under the front seat and pulled out the drugs I'd stashed there, I knew it was over. I had wrapped my note in an elastic around them.

As soon as he saw the drugs, Brady's mouth

dropped open. Jake unwrapped the note from the elastic and started reading it out. Then Brady took off.

I tossed the binoculars on the seat next to me as I watched him run across the parking lot. Because Jake had been on the passenger side of the Mustang and Brady had already moved about twenty feet from the car, he had a head start on my boyfriend. I was pretty sure Jake could catch him.

But I was betting Queenie could do it faster.

I immediately started the car, threw it into gear, and jammed my foot against the gas pedal. Queenie pealed out of her parking spot, tires squealing. Brady was running away from me, so he couldn't see that it was me in the car coming up behind him.

I was catching up to Brady, and fast. He would have heard Queenie's engine, no doubt about it, but he must have thought it was Jake in the police cruiser. He turned to the right just before I reached him, trying to escape, but I swung the steering wheel to stay with him.

After all, if I hit him with the car just a little bit, that was fine. It's not *really* running someone over if you just clip them.

But with Brady changing direction to try and get away, I was risking too much if I actually tried to hit him. Instead, I reached over into the cupholder, grabbed my still-almost-full coffee, and hurled it out the window as I passed him.

Randy Johnson couldn't have thrown more accurately. The iced mocha exploded against Brady's head, drenching him in sticky coffee and ice. He lost his balance and fell to the pavement with a shout. About ten seconds later, Jake caught up to him.

"Stay down," Jake ordered, pressing a foot on Brady's back as he slapped the cuffs on him. "You're under arrest."

"I didn't do anything," Brady protested as soon as Jake finished reading him his Miranda rights.

"That brick of cocaine under the seat says otherwise."

"That bitch put it there."

"And what bitch would that be?"

"The one who left the note. Charlie. Charlie Gibson. All of this is her fault."

"Sure it is. You're saying some lady left a brick of cocaine in your car and that you have no idea at all what it's about. The jury's going to *love* that story."

"It's true. And you hit me with that coffee. That's harassment. Cops aren't supposed to do that shit." Brady's tone was quickly going from angry to whiny. He obviously didn't even realize I was there. In the chaos of everything, he wouldn't have seen Queenie and must have still thought it was Jake in the cruiser who had come after him.

I grinned to myself and sat on Queenie's hood while Jake walked Brady back toward the cruiser.

"Wait," I heard Brady say. "If your car's over there, who hit me?"

He spun around, and his gaze landed directly on mine. I flashed him the sweetest smile I could and gave him a finger wave.

"That's her!" Brady shouted. "That's the bitch who left the coke in my car. You have to believe me! That's her!"

"You'll have lots of time to tell this story when we get you booked," Jake said.

"She's the bitch who's framing me! You have to talk to her!" Brady struggled as if he was trying to break free of Jake's grasp to come and talk to me, but Jake knew what he was doing. He shoved Brady, kicking and screaming, into the back of the police cruiser. When he was safely locked in, Jake grabbed an evidence bag, placed the bundle of cocaine inside it, and walked over toward me.

"Thanks," I said. "I really appreciate it."

"He should be going to jail for a long time. That's definitely a message you left for him."

Jake unfolded the letter, and I saw my own writing scribbled on the page in Sharpie.

This is a message for the Ham gang: if you come near me again, I will slit your throat, cut your abdomen open, and slurp your intestines like spaghetti, using your blood for sauce.

Oh, and then I'll go to Seattle and fuck your dad.

Leave me alone. This is your last warning.

XOXO Charlie

Jake raised an eyebrow. "You're going to slurp their intestines like spaghetti? That's certainly a mental image."

"I can't believe that of everything written there, *that's* the part you have a problem with," I replied with a grin.

"I mean, I'm assuming you're not *actually* going to go bang their dad."

"No. But the gang is dangerous. That's what makes them intimidating. Everyone knows they're willing to go to great lengths to destroy the people they have beefs with. So I figure I'm going to go even crazier. Because there's nothing more terrifying than someone who comes off as being so unhinged you don't know what they're going to do. And if I can leave a message that talks about slurping intestines like spaghetti and then signing it like *Gossip Girl*, I figure that's going to get them a little off kilter. I'm not the same woman who saw a finger on my doorstep and ran halfway across the Pacific Ocean to get away from them. And I want them to know that. I want them to wonder, when they get off that plane, if they're going to leave Hawaii alive."

"Well, this letter will do that. When they get the message out, anyway. Brady is going to jail, and I expect even with this letter in evidence, he's going to be put away for a long time."

"What if you didn't put the letter into the bag?" I suggested.

"Are you asking me to destroy evidence of a crime?"

"I am, but not for nothing. Think about it. If Brady sees you talking to me then sees you tearing up that letter and pretending you've never heard about it, what message does that send? It tells them that I'm working with the police already. It adds another layer of instability. But I'm not going to pressure you on this. I know you're a rule follower, and I do respect that."

"Do you really?" Jake's voice dripped with skepticism.

"I do, ultimately. I might not like it, and I think it's dumb, especially when so many other cops seem to pick and choose what laws they follow, but I do think your adherence speaks to your character. Still, I think it would be a net good not only for society but also for me personally if you chose to do this."

Jake's eyes met mine. They were like dark pools. I couldn't tell what he was thinking.

Finally, he held the paper in front of me and tore it in half. Then in half again, and again, his eyes not leaving mine.

"You're right," he finally said. "I became a cop because I wanted people to get justice. I became a cop because people like my sister had no options. And most of the time, we get there after a crime has been committed. Justice has to come in the form of punishment. But isn't true justice really in prevention?"

I swallowed hard. The fact that Jake was willing to do this for me meant so much. "Thank you," I said quietly.

"You can't mention this to anyone."

"I won't. I promise. I know what you just did and how important it was."

"Now Brady has no defense. He's going to yell and scream about this letter, and I'm going to insist it doesn't exist."

"It's not gaslighting if they deserve it," I said, the corner of my mouth curling up into a small smile.

"Sometimes, I feel like you're going to end up in the back of my police car one day."

"Not a chance, babe. I use my insanity for good."

"Where on earth did you get a whole brick of coke, anyway?"

"Vesper stole it while we were looking into another case."

"Do I want to know more details?"

"Definitely not."

Jake sighed. "Okay. I'm going to go take Brady in," he said, sealing the bag of cocaine. He handed me the shreds of paper. "Get rid of this, okay?"

"I will. Thanks for helping me. They're not going to be thrilled that one of the top-level gang members has been tricked into spending ten years in jail, either. I hope that's going to convince them that I'm serious."

Jake nodded. "I hope so too. Let me know if you hear anything else about them."

"I will."

I wanted to reach over and pull Jake into a hug, but I knew Brady was watching. It was better that he think this relationship was strictly professional.

"I'll talk to you later."

Jake turned and walked back toward the car. As he opened the door to the cruiser, I could already hear Brady's whiny voice, a note of panic in it.

"You tore up that letter! What the fuck, man? That was evidence I'm innocent. She framed me!"

I turned and climbed back into Queenie. Brady had been arrested, and he would pass the message I'd left on to the Ham brothers: I was not someone to be messed with, and if they tried it, they were in for a world of hurt.

Chapter 26

With Brady out of the way, I had to take care of the murder investigation. I sent a quick text and received an answer a few minutes later. I was going to meet with Lily and see if I could get her to admit she had killed Tony.

Of course, I didn't mention that in my text.

Lily was at work and suggested we meet behind the main shopping area in Kahului, where there was a handful of smaller buildings with options for lunch and plenty of seating at picnic tables outside. It was a quiet part of town, especially in the midafternoon after the lunch rush, and we would have plenty of privacy to have our chat.

That was fine with me, especially since I was already at that end of the island. I went to our meeting spot and ordered a plate lunch with Spam musubi on the side—mainlanders tended to avoid

Spam, but here in Hawaii, it was practically a local delicacy—and dug in and considered my case while I waited for Lily to show up.

Eating always helped me think.

She arrived about twenty minutes later, just as I was finishing up. I motioned for her to go inside and order, and she returned soon afterward with a drink.

"I'm not really hungry," Lily said. "But I didn't want to meet at the office. I didn't want everyone there to see me crying. They already give me such sad looks. My boss told me I could go home, but in a way, it's easier to get my mind off it if I try and distract myself, you know?"

"I do," I replied. "After all, I imagine you must relive it over and over in your head, right? What it looked like when you murdered Tony? Seeing his blood in the water, like a shark had just taken his life? When really, the shark was you."

Lily's eyes flew to mine. "What are you talking about?"

"I know, Lily. I know the truth. He used you from the start, didn't he? And you had absolutely no idea. He didn't love you. He just wanted your kidney."

I paused and let my words sink in. Then, Lily laughed, a high-pitched, humorless sound with just a touch of insanity in it. "So you figured it out, did you? All right. You got me. I was sure I was going to get away with it too. But you're right. I did kill Tony, and I can't stop thinking about it. I thought it would be easy. After all, he fucked me out of a kidney. Can you imagine what it must take to do something like that to someone? The level of psychopath you would have to be to find somebody and pretend to love them just so you could have one of their organs? I could have *died*. I was willing to take that risk for him because he loved me. But no. He didn't love me. He loved my tissue-match results. How did you figure it out, though? Am I going to be arrested?"

I shrugged. "I'm not sure yet. I'm not a cop."

Okay, that was a lie. I did know she was going to be arrested. I was recording everything she said. The fact of the matter was, murderers went to jail.

I took a breath and continued. "It started at the hospital. You were there to get tested to see if your tissues were a match with your cousin's, which they weren't. Tony was there getting regular dialysis. He knew how everything worked because he was at the hospital so often. And at some point, he saw your test results. They were probably in a pile near the desk. Had he been checking them regularly whenever the desk was unattended? I suspect yes. But finally, he found one that matched. But he couldn't just ask you for a kidney. You were a stranger. You weren't going to say yes. He had to get you to like him. And a man like Tony, he was used to making women feel special."

"I was such an idiot," Lily muttered.

"No, you weren't. He was older, he was experienced in doing this, and you had no way to realize that was his M.O."

"People told me when I started getting close to him. I thought they were wrong. They didn't know Tony like I did, I told myself. He was different. He never showed any signs of cheating. And he was so sweet. He helped pay for my cousin's treatment. He actually listened to me. Do you know how many dates I've been on where I felt like I was just talking into the void? Tony wasn't like that at all, and I genuinely fell in love with him."

"So you gave him your kidney. How long after that did you find out about the cheating?"

"Three months. A woman came up to me and told me she had been dating Tony, and she hadn't realized he was seeing someone else at the time. She told me if it was her, she'd want to know. We were both dating him. I didn't believe her, so she showed me some pictures on her phone. They were definitely together. I called her a liar and ran away. I wish I hadn't. I wish I knew who she was, because while I was mad at her at the time, she did me a favor. She helped me see who he really was.

"And the worst was, I saw the time stamp on some of the photos. They were dated just before we met. He was already with her when we met. He was with her when he asked me to give him a kidney. I was nothing to him."

Tears welled in Lily's eyes, and she stared blankly at the picnic table in front of us, picking idly at a splinter of wood. "I meant it the other day when I said that I knew giving Tony a kidney didn't mean we'd be together forever. I understood things might not work out between us. But this was different, you know? This wasn't us separating after the donation for whatever reason. He had known the entire time. From the day we met, he had been with this other woman. And that was the betrayal."

"Yeah. I can't really say I blame you. So when you found out, what did you do? Did you confront Tony?"

"No. I wasn't sure what I wanted to do. So I kept the knowledge to myself. I pretended it didn't happen. I tried to convince myself it was all in my head. But of course, that wasn't true. So then, I decided I was going to do the next-best thing. If Tony thought he was going to get my kidney for free, he was wrong."

"You put the camera in his bedroom. Someone mentioned to me that you worked in IT. Connecting it to a Bluetooth device wouldn't have been hard."

"That's right. I specifically set it up so it would have looked like someone just poked their phone camera through the window. And before I sent the first photos, I removed the camera, just in case. I put it back again later. I sent him pictures of his other girlfriend, saying that if he didn't pay, I'd tell Lily. It was easy. I got my money."

"How much?"

"About forty grand in total. Is that what a kidney goes for on the black market? Probably something like that. Anyway, I knew Tony didn't have much more money than that, so my gravy train was coming to an end. But I wasn't satisfied. He literally took an organ from me. He had to pay."

"So you decided to kill him."

"I did. I chose the surfing competition for a few reasons. One, that early in the morning, it would still be a little bit dark when everyone got on the water. It would be easy to do it without being noticed. Everyone would be focused on their own waves. And everyone on the water that day would have known Tony. That opened up the suspect pool significantly. Not that I wanted someone else to go down for my crime. I just wanted there to be enough suspects that I wouldn't immediately be considered. After all, everyone always looks to the girlfriend."

I nodded. "Yeah."

"But the thing is, none of the men understood."

"That's how I got there," I said. "I realized over and over, women were telling me what kind of person Tony was, but all the men were saying he changed. But do people really change? Especially overnight like that? With some effort, sure. But this seemed like a lot. So I tried to figure out what this case would look like if I assumed that all the women telling me he was a cheater through and through were telling me the truth. And I realized that must have been the betrayal. You knew he was cheating. And you were getting your revenge."

"Damn straight."

"So that morning, while Tony was chatting to people, you got your knife ready."

"It was almost too easy. I had a neoprene suit on, since I run cold, and I shoved the knife into the waist and put a loose rash guard over it. I swam out, following Tony. At one point, he caught a wave, and I followed him. When he started paddling back out into the ocean, another wave came toward us, and that was my chance. I shoved the knife right in his back. He had just enough time to see what happened, and he looked at me as he died. Then he collapsed onto the board, and I took off, letting it bob back to the shore. That was it. I paddled back out and kept surfing until I saw the commotion on shore, and I knew he'd been found."

"Do you regret what you did?"

"No. He deserved it. He played with my heart to get at my kidneys, knowing the entire time that he was two-timing me." Lily's gaze shifted to the edge of the table. "I guess I kind of feel bad about what I did, in a way. I never thought I was a murderer. But he killed a part of me too. How can I ever trust someone again, knowing what he did? So many people warned me, and I didn't listen.

"Well, it's done, now. Tony is dead. And you're the only person who figured it out. What are you going to do?"

"I don't know," I lied. I was going straight to the cops. Did I feel bad for Lily? Yes, of course I did. She had been betrayed by someone she loved. But that happened to plenty of people, and most of them didn't immediately resort to blackmail and premeditated murder as a revenge strategy.

"Obviously, I understand why you did it. Vesper is my client, and the police haven't found evidence that she's the killer. So I think I can forget we ever had this conversation."

Lily breathed a sigh of relief, her shoulders relaxing. "Thank you, Charlie. I'm glad you understand."

"Just try not to kill anyone else, okay?" I asked with a smile.

"I think I've done more than enough of that for one lifetime," Lily replied.

I said goodbye and took my dishes back inside. When I emerged, Lily had gone. Oh, well. She wouldn't be hard to find. I just had to get back to the police station and give the recording on my phone to Jake. I pulled out my phone while I was still in the shade of the awning in front of the building, stopped the recording, and emailed it to him.

I hoped he was going to get over the fact that I had solved this crime before he did. The fact that I'd just handed him a killer on a silver platter would hopefully go a long way toward that.

I sent a quick text to Dot and Rosie as well, keeping them apprised of the situation.

As I walked out into the parking lot toward Queenie, at the other end of the lot, Jake called.

"Hello?" I answered.

"Is this recording what I think it is?"

"Sure is. You can feel free to pick up Lily at your earliest convenience. She's your killer, and you've got everything you need on there."

"Where are you now?"

"Still in Kahului. We met for lunch at that little outdoor mall with the Hawaiian place that does good spam musubi."

Suddenly, out of the corner of my eye, I saw a car careening toward me. The engine revved as it flew at me. I didn't even have a chance to think. I just reacted.

Tires squealed as I dove out of the way. My phone clattered against the ground as I rolled to the side, narrowly avoiding the tires of the car that had just tried to hit me.

"Charlie?" Jake's voice called through the phone

speaker a few feet away. "Charlie, are you okay? What's going on?"

"Looks like Lily isn't going to stop at just one murder," I shouted as she slammed on the brakes and squealed to a stop.

The reverse lights came on, and a second later, the car came at me from the other side. I darted in the other direction, back toward the store, but Lily was too fast in the car. She drove at me, and while I tried to swerve to avoid her at the last second, this time, she clipped me. I fell to the ground, pain coursing through my hip.

"Shit," I muttered, crawling toward Queenie. This would have been a great time to have a James Bond–style missile-firing system built into my car. I wondered if Olivia would be willing to install for me. If I made it out of here alive, that was.

I was too exposed here. Lily was getting ready to take me out for good. Queenie was at least fifty feet away. I was never going to get to her without being hit again, not with my hip in so much pain. Maybe I should have hit Brady with my car earlier after all. He deserved to hurt this much.

It would be cruelly ironic if this was how I was going to die.

No, I refused to think that way. I wasn't going to die. I just had to get to Queenie. There was another car about twenty feet away. I ran to it, limping heavily, every step I took feeling as though I'd just been stabbed. Lily came after me, but I used the car as a shield.

"You don't have to do this," I shouted. "You're not getting away with it."

"This isn't my car. It won't get traced to me," she called out in reply. As if there weren't dozens of witnesses in the nearby stores who could probably see what was going on. "Just come out, and I promise I'll make it quick."

"Sorry, not today."

I was standing behind the car, and she was in front of it. I moved to the left, and Lily slammed on the gas. At the last second, I darted right, which sent a pain so fierce up my leg that the edges of my vision went dark for a second. But I forced myself to stay with it. If I passed out now, I was screwed.

Lily jerked the wheel to try and hit me, but instead, she hit the car. This was exactly what I'd hoped for. It wouldn't incapacitate her, but it stunned her for long enough that her car was stopped for a few seconds.

I limped to the passenger side of the older sedan and launched myself through the open window of her car.

"What the hell?" Lily screamed. She slammed on the gas, flying into reverse, while I grabbed at the steering wheel. I didn't even care if we crashed at this point. I just knew that while I was in this car, she couldn't hit me with it.

About five seconds later, the car slammed into the building behind us. I gasped as I was pressed hard into the seat. My awkward position, half in the car and half out, spread across the passenger seat, was not an ideal place to be in a car crash.

The air bag exploded, although I heard it more than I saw it.

After a couple seconds, I realized I was alive. I reached over and grabbed the keys from Lily's car, cutting the engine, then squirmed my way awkwardly back out. A few employees emerged from the building Lily had just hit, mouths agape as they took in the scene.

"She's trying to kill me," I shouted, running back into the restaurant for protection.

Looking out, I saw Lily slamming her steering wheel in frustration while one of the employees pulled out a phone to call the police.

It was over.

Chapter 27

The police arrived within about two minutes. They had already been on their way; Jake had called the Kahului station from Kihei. As soon as they arrived on the scene, they took Lily into custody. All the fight seemed to have gone out of her. There was no way she was getting away with it now.

I went to find my phone, which had been run over at some point. Luckily, for Christmas, Zoe had bought me a "Charlie-proof" phone case. Supposedly, the manufacturer tested these cases by dropping them from a helicopter onto concrete to see if the phones survived.

When I tapped the screen, it lit up. Wow. I was going to have to thank Zoe again for that gift. I called Jake, who answered on the first ring.

"Charlie?"

"Yeah."

"Are you okay?"

"I'm fine. Okay, I'm alive, at least. And I still have all my limbs. Lily is under arrest."

Jake let out a jagged breath on the other end of the line. "Thank goodness. I'm so glad you're okay. I'm on my way now. I left as soon as I called the cops.s"

"Okay. I'll talk to you soon."

"Charlie?"

"Yeah?"

"I'm glad you're safe."

"Me too."

I ended the call and sat at the same picnic table where I'd just interviewed Lily. I steadied my breathing, trying to get the adrenaline to pass. My hip was killing me. I was going to have to go to the hospital. I knew that. But I wanted to speak to Jake first.

About ten minutes later, he peeled into the parking lot, driving his new car. He must have broken every speed limit to get here this fast. He jumped out of the car and ran to me as fast as he could, immediately taking me into a huge bear hug.

Pressing my face into his chest, he ran his hands over my hair, resting his chin on the top of my head and holding me close to him. "I'm so glad you're okay."

"I'm fine," I insisted. "And I found the killer."

"You did. She tried to kill you?"

"I let my guard down," I admitted. "I basically let her believe that I wasn't going to turn her in. I thought that would be enough, but she tried to run me over as I was heading back to Queenie."

"Do you need to go to the hospital?"

"I think so, yeah. Can we take Queenie? But you drive. The passenger seat is higher and will be easier to get into."

"Yeah, of course," Jake said.

I went to grab my keys, and then I paused. I didn't want to have this conversation. I wasn't good at hard talks. But if Jake and I were going to be a couple, and if this relationship was going to work, it had to happen.

And the more time I spent with him, the more I realized I did want this to work out. Maybe not forever, but at least for now.

"Before we go though, we need to talk. About how you're jealous of the fact that I'm a better investigator than you."

Jake tilted his head to the side. "What?"

"You've been cold to me for days. This whole case. You practically yelled at me the other day when I suggested working together to solve this case because you didn't think I was taking it in the right direction. Well, I was right. I'm good at this job, Jake. You're going to have to come to grips with that."

Jake's mouth opened slightly as he furrowed his

brow. "Wait. You think I'm jealous of how good you are at this? You think that's the problem?"

"Yeah. I mean, that's it, isn't it? We could have worked on this together. We might have solved it faster. But at every turn, you pushed me away because you couldn't handle how much closer I was to it."

"Wow. I'm not sure what's more insulting: the fact that you think I'm that bad at my own job or the fact that you think I'm so toxic that I would take it personally if you were better at this than me."

I stared at him. "So it's not jealousy?"

"No, Charlie. I'm not jealous of what you've done. I'm glad you solved this. The important thing is that the killer was found."

"Then why have you been pushing me away this whole time?"

Jake ran a hand through his hair before answering. "Because, Charlie, I saw the body. I know what this killer did. And knowing that you were out there, hunting them down, putting yourself in danger, it honestly scares the crap out of me."

"You knew this was my job," I said. "I've done it before."

"I know. And I thought I would be okay with it right from the start. I know you're good at this, but at the same time, I know you're willing to put yourself in danger to get to the bottom of a case. Your devotion to finding a killer is admirable, but every time I saw you, every time you told me what you were up to, I couldn't help but wonder if you were next. And I couldn't handle it. So yeah, I pushed you away. But not because I was jealous. Because I'm terrified of losing you."

"Oh." I didn't know what else to say.

"So yes, I pushed you away. Because like an idiot, I thought if maybe I kept you away from my investigation, you might keep away from the killer."

I paused. This conversation had veered off the nearest exit and was coming into a collision course with emotions I didn't want to have to deal with. "But I didn't."

"No," Jake admitted. "You kept going, and you found the killer. And don't get me wrong—I'm thrilled you did. But I'm also scared shitless. When I heard you scream and heard the phone drop and a crunch, I didn't know what had happened. And then you told me, and…"

Jake took a deep breath to steady himself. I hadn't realized. He wasn't jealous. He was scared. Scared for me.

He continued. "Do you know how I felt when I heard that? I thought I was going to lose you. I thought you were going to die, and there was nothing I could do about it. That I was going to get a call telling me there was a body in Kahului, and it was going to be you. And that I was thirty minutes away. Too far away to save you."

There was silence between us for a few seconds, then I spoke. "You don't have to save me. I know your history. I know your history with your sister. But I'm not her. You're not going to be able to stop me from getting into trouble. So you're either going to have to come to grips with that, or this isn't going to work. Because I'm not willing to pull back on the way I'm living my life."

"You don't want to be put in a cage."

"Exactly."

"I know. I knew that going into this. And I don't want to. But I care about you, Charlie. I know how dangerous these situations are. I thought I'd handle it better. I didn't. But I'm a work in progress. We all are."

"I don't know. I think I'm pretty perfect as is," I replied, cracking a small smile to break the tension. My joke didn't ease the weight of the giant stone that had just settled in my stomach.

"Okay, *I* am a work in progress. I don't want to give up on this relationship. But I need to figure out how to handle working the same cases as you better, knowing what I know about murder, about murderers. Look at us. We're sitting here, having this conversation after you've been hit by a car. This is all new to me. I've never had a girlfriend who's this…"

"Insane?" I offered.

"That's probably the right word for it, frankly. I just don't know where to go from here."

"We work together," I said. "You've said it yourself: you're afraid of me getting in too deep, into too much trouble. This happened because I took it on by myself. You needed to let me in. If we had worked this together, not only would we possibly have figured it out sooner, but you could have been here. Maybe not talking to Lily, but you could have been around. And she probably still would have tried to hit me with the car, but you could have stopped it faster. I think that airbag crushed my spine."

Jake shook his head. "Okay, we're going to the hospital now. Maybe you're right. Maybe that's what I have to do. Learn to let you in a bit more. But I have regulations I need to follow too."

"I'm not asking you to break the law. Okay, sometimes I ask you to break the law. But mostly, I'm just asking you not to put up a wall every time our jobs have us in the same place."

"I know. And I'm going to work on it. Now, come on. You need to get to the hospital."

SIX HOURS LATER, I WAS BACK HOME, LYING ON THE couch, my new accessory—a cast on my leg—propped up on the coffee table. Lily had broken my tibia when she'd hit me with the car. Luckily, the break was about as good as it gets when it comes to your leg snapping in half, and I wasn't going to need surgery. Just some rest and moving around on crutches for a few weeks before I could change to a moon boot.

Jake took great care of me, driving me to the hospital and then home, but once I was back, he had to go to the police station to deal with Lily. Promising him that I would be fine, I called Dot, who announced that she and Rosie would be there shortly.

Dot arrived first, immediately heading to the fridge.

"Want anything?"

"No, I'm good, thanks," I replied. "The hospital gave me some painkillers that have me feeling pretty great."

Just then, there came a knock at the door. Dot strode over to answer it and let in Rosie, who had a small carrier with her. Inside it, a dark void with big, yellow eyes stared out at me.

Coco, who was cuddling with me on the couch, sniffed the air a couple of times, obviously aware of our new visitor. Luckily, she had never been the kind of dog to chase cats, and she went right back to sleep.

"Who is this?" I asked with a smile as I looked at the crate.

"I'm calling her Threat Level Midnight," Rosie said. "Middie for short. I spent all of last night waiting for her. She eventually made an appearance at seven this morning. I left my balcony door open with a few slices of ham on the counter, and sure enough, she eventually showed up. I followed her and found her stash. You were right, Charlie. The culprit was the cat."

"Threat Level Midnight, huh?" I knew Rosie loved American pop culture; it was one of the reasons she'd moved here. And this was a great name for a cat.

"It fits. She was a crafty one, but I caught her. I wanted to show you, since I figure you won't be moving around much these next few weeks. Are you all right?"

"I've had worse. I'll be fine."

"You're a tough cookie, I'll give you that," Dot said.

"And Brady isn't going to be a problem anymore. I took care of him." I ran through what had happened that morning.

Dot chuckled. "That explains why the GPS tag I had on the car showed it in the Maui PD impound lot. I guess it's time to disable that tag. I don't think the idiots in their IT department will be able to track it back to me, but you never know, and I'd rather not have them asking too many questions."

"What are you going to do with the cat?" I asked Rosie.

She peered into the carrier, and Middie let out a small meow, which made Coco's ears twitch.

"I think I might keep her. I respect her hustle. She needs a home, and she already knows my complex. My apartment won't be a big change for her. And I promised her I'll never abandon her like her previous owners did."

"She can be our mascot," I said with a smile.

Middie meowed at me in reply.

Epilogue

The following weekend, I was back on the beach, although this time, I had crutches and a fold-out chair.

"I'm going to get sand in my cast," I whined as I made my way down to the beach, my speed hindered by the crutches.

"Well, you should have dodged that car, then," Zoe replied, refusing to give my whining any sort of sympathy.

"I found a murderer. Besides, that's not even the worst part of this."

"What is?" Henry asked as he carried a bag full of Zoe's things along with my chair.

"Now that I've had to pull out of the competition, I'm out of the running to win the year's supply of pie."

Zoe laughed. "Truly, a tragedy for the ages."

"If you win the raffle, I'm totally going to steal the prize off you."

"I promise to share my pie if I win," Zoe said with a grin.

"You go on and get warmed up," Henry told her. "We'll hold down the fort over here."

"Thanks, babe," Zoe said, giving him a quick kiss.

"Oooooooooh," I said.

When Zoe pulled away, she glared at me. "We talked about this. Stop being your mother, or I'm going to leave you here at the beach."

"You wouldn't dare."

"Try me."

"Fine. I'll be less weird about this. But for the record, you two would make adorable babies."

"Annnnd that's my cue to head down to the water," Zoe said. "I'll see you soon. Henry, there are some sleeping pills in my bag. Please don't hesitate to use them on Charlie if she gets too annoying."

"I'm adorable," I called out to her as Zoe ran toward the water, her board under her arm.

Henry opened my chair for me and motioned for me to sit. "It's good of you to come and support her, even though you can't compete today," he said.

"Oh, I'm much happier sitting in a chair on the sand. In fact, if there was no sand, it would be even better. But I want to watch Zoe win. She's a good surfer."

"She works hard at it," Henry agreed. "I brought snacks. I know it's early, but do you want some?"

"I always knew you were a great guy," I replied. He pulled out a bag of trail mix, and I began picking the M&Ms out of it. "Do you surf?"

"A little bit here and there. She's better at it than I am, though."

"You should have entered this competition to win the free pie."

Henry laughed. "And donated it to you if I won?"

"Now you're getting it."

After a while, Vesper came out of the water. I waved.

She came over to sit down on the sand next to us. "I haven't had a chance to thank you," Vesper said. "Jake told me you're the one who broke this case open."

I nodded. "I told you I'd get to the bottom of it."

"And now you get to learn what it's like to be me for a few weeks for your trouble," she said, motioning to my cast. She glanced at Henry. "Did your thing with the uh, other stuff go well?"

"Yup. I'm hoping that I'm not going to hear anything from the people giving me trouble anymore."

"Me too. You're a good kid, Charlie."

"Thanks, Vesper. I'm just glad you're not in jail."

"So am I."

She gave Henry a nod then got up. "I have to get ready for my heat."

"You're going to crush it," I said warmly.

"Always do."

Vesper left, and I watched as Zoe began paddling back toward shore as well. Things were pretty good. Okay, I hadn't won the pie. But I'd solved a murder. Brady Ludlam was in jail, facing drug charges. Rosie had a new cat. And sure, I had sand in my cast. But all things considered, it could have been a lot worse.

LATER THAT AFTERNOON, AFTER ALL THE MAIN awards had been given out, I was admiring Zoe's trophy for winning the nineteen-to-twenty-nine category for the last time.

"I said you were going to win this," I told her. "Now you're moving up in the world. Can you win the thirty-to-thirty-nine category ten years running?"

Zoe laughed. "I highly doubt that."

"I think she can," Henry said, wrapping an arm around her. "I believe in you."

"Thanks," Zoe replied, a flush crawling up her face.

Then, the intermittent voice over the loud-speaker that had been announcing the raffle prizes spoke.

"Next up, we've got one year of free pies to give away thanks to our sponsors, Kihei Pie Company. One lucky surfer is going to be very well fed going into this year. And the winner is… well, I don't think I need to give a last name, since we all know the best-looking lady on the island with only one leg. It's Vesper!"

Cheers rose from the crowd as Vesper made her way to the stage, where the draw was held. She motioned to the man to give her the mic, which he did.

"First of all, Ryan, thank you. But one leg is all I need to kick your ass if you ever imply I'm not the best-looking woman on this island, period," she said with a good-natured grin.

A call of "oooooh," rose from the crowd, and Ryan held his hands up in front of him in surrender, a sheepish grin on his face.

"Secondly," Vesper continued, "I want to give my prize to someone who couldn't compete today because of me. I know she hasn't said anything to anyone here, but she had her leg broken in the process of solving Tony's murder, and it's thanks to her that Lily is behind bars today. I can't think of anyone who deserves this more. Come on up here, Charlie. Come and get your pie."

Zoe put two fingers in her mouth and whistled as more cheers rose from the crowd. The clapping was louder than any I'd heard before as I walked up with the help of my crutches and got the little plastic card entitling me to unlimited pie for a whole year.

Okay, this was worth getting sand in my cast.

BOOK 8 - MAI TAI MASSACRE: WHEN A LOCAL Maui resort is attacked, it's all hands on deck to try and find the culprit. Which means Charlie is on the case, but so is Jake. And the last time they worked the same case was choppier than the north shore waves during a storm surge.

But Charlie's got more to worry about than just solving this case. For one thing, why has her mom been acting strangely? And have the Ham brothers in Seattle gotten the message to leave her alone?

Charlie could really use another drink, but she's going to have to keep a clear head if she's going to get to the bottom of this case. The killer thinks they've gotten away with it, and the closer Charlie gets to uncovering the truth, the more danger she's in. Can she bring the killer to justice before they make sure it's last call for Charlie?

Click here now to pre-order Mai Tai Massacre, coming July 2023

About the Author

Jasmine Webb is a thirty-something who lives in the mountains most of the year, dreaming of the beach. When she's not writing stories you can find her chasing her old dog around, hiking up moderately-sized hills, or playing Pokemon Go.

Want to find out how Dot and Rosie met? Sign up for Jasmine's newsletter to get that story, and be the first to find out about new releases here: http://www.authorjasminewebb.com/newsletter

You can also connect with her on other social media here:

Also by Jasmine Webb

Charlotte Gibson Mysteries

Aloha Alibi

Maui Murder

Beachside Bullet

Pina Colada Poison

Hibiscus Homicide

Kalikimaka Killer

Surfboard Stabbing

Mai Tai Massacre (coming July 2023)

Poppy Perkins Mysteries

Booked for Murder

Read Between the Lies

On the Slayed Page (coming April 2023)

Made in the USA
Middletown, DE
31 July 2023